"I don't give up so easily," he said

There was something in the way he said the words that was more frightening than a nightmare.

Dear God, Siana thought, *the man's insane. He's a madman and I'm standing here talking to him and any minute now he'll come in and there's nothing I can do to stop him.*

"Please go away," she whispered.

"I want to talk to you first. I think I can help you."

"Help me," she croaked. "Help me?" She wanted to laugh but couldn't.

"Yes. To get your memory back," he said.

Dark waves came rushing into her head, filling her senses, drowning her. She thought she was going to faint. How did he know? How *could* he know that she had lost her memory?

Many of these titles are available at your local bookseller.

For a free catalogue listing all available Harlequin Romances,
send your name and address to:

HARLEQUIN READER SERVICE,
M.P.O. Box 707, Niagara Falls, N.Y. 14302
Canadian address: Stratford, Ontario, Canada N5A 6W2

With This Ring

by

MARY WIBBERLEY

Harlequin Books

TORONTO • LONDON • NEW YORK • AMSTERDAM
SYDNEY • HAMBURG • PARIS • STOCKHOLM

Original hardcover edition published in 1979
by Mills & Boon Limited

ISBN 0-373-02316-2

Harlequin edition published February 1980

Printed in U.S.A.

CHAPTER ONE

SHE walked along the beach every day, gathering driftwood for the fire, but today was different from others, because Aunt Peggy and Uncle Peter had gone to relatives in Canada on holiday, and she was alone in the house. Siana stretched her arms, as if at a sense of freedom, and thought about them. They would be on the plane now, winging across the Atlantic, probably wondering how she was getting on alone. They had been very doubtful about leaving her, had urged her to go too, but she had refused. They were kind, and she loved them dearly for the way they had cared for her ever since the accident, but she was looking forward to being alone. Free to get up and go to bed when she pleased, free to eat or not to eat—free to read, and to be quiet.

She had a bundle of sticks in her arms, and it was enough for the one day. She liked to hear the salty wood crackle and spit in the fireplace and see the flames dancing, because sometimes, in them, she caught glimpses of fragments of memories, not unpleasant, and she wondered at those times if she would ever remember the past again, if she would ever know anything of her life before the accident. The doctors and the psychiatrists said it was possible—but she had seen in their eyes what they did not say: that they thought it highly unlikely.

She climbed steadily over the sand dunes, wondering if any of the wood was worth saving to paint. Driftwood came in odd shapes, and sometimes she had polished and painted a particularly shaped piece, and it assumed a life of its own and became a perching bird or a running dog....

'Good afternoon.' The deep voice came from nearby, and she turned, starting, nearly dropping the wood. She had been so lost in thought that she hadn't even seen the man approach.

'Good afternoon.' She had seen him once or twice before, in the distance, gathering wood as she did, or looking along the beach for pebbles. She didn't know him, had never seen him close to, but now she did, and a pulse of fear beat in her throat. He was a big man, and he wore rough seamen's clothes, and a peaked cap. He carried a sack. When he smiled, his face was pleasant, the hard features softening and becoming gentler, his eyes creasing into laughter lines. He was a darkly attractive man, and strong-looking.

'I'm sorry if I startled you, but we seem to be on a similar mission.' He lifted the sack. 'Both collecting wood. There's enough of it.'

'Yes.' She continued looking at him, because she didn't know what else to do. It would be rude to move away abruptly, as she was tempted. Yet she didn't want to speak to him, because for some reason she didn't understand, he frightened her.

'You live in the village?'

'Yes—just outside. Excuse me, I must go now. I——'

'Got to get back? Mind if I walk along with you? It's very quiet here, isn't it?'

Siana answered the last question first, although she wasn't sure if he expected answers to any. 'Yes, it is quiet.' She began to move, soft-footed, sure of her movements in spite of the limp, because she knew every inch of the sand dunes, she walked them every day. He fell into step beside her.

'You live in the big house, don't you?'

'How do you know? You just asked me if I lived in the village. If you already knew, why did you ask?'

His eyes narrowed. 'I was making polite conversation. I thought everyone was friendly round here——' he shrugged. 'However, if you don't want to talk——'

There was no one in sight. Behind them the sea and the empty beach, around them the rolling hills of sand dunes and tussocks of grass, and ahead, the trees. Siana felt unreasoning panic rise in her and her instinct was to run, but he looked as though he could run a lot faster. It would be best to keep quite calm—and keep on walking. 'I don't mind,' she said. 'It's just that I'm not used to seeing other people out here. I—I like to be alone.'

'So do I—at times. But not always. Here, let me carry your wood for you. It looks heavy.'

She clutched it to her. 'It's not. It's fine.'

'I won't pinch it.' He sounded amused. 'I've enough of my own.'

'I like carrying it,' she said, knowing it sounded stupid even as she said it. And it wasn't easy. She wished she had thought to bring a sack, like him. She wished her limp didn't get worse when she was nervous.

'Suit yourself.' They were approaching the belt of trees now and her heart beat faster. How did you say—I'm frightened of you and I don't want to go any further with you? There was no way it could be said. She wished her aunt and uncle hadn't gone. She wished they were at home waiting for her, so that she would feel safe, but the house was empty. She hadn't even locked the door when she went out, because people didn't in these parts. She wasn't even sure where the key was. And if anything happened to her, no one would know about it for three weeks—and somehow it would be like the last time, even though she couldn't remember it, she only knew what little she had been told.

'Your name's Siana, isn't it?' He even pronounced it correctly, Sharna, as though someone had told him—as though he had *asked*—and she stared at him, wide-eyed, and it was all there on her face for him to see.

'Oh no——' he said softly. 'Oh *no*! Do I terrify you so?'

She didn't answer. She didn't need to. If she ran, and he ran after her, she would only get a few yards, because her leg had been weak ever since the accident, and although there were no outward scars she could not run far without it letting her down.

'You're safe,' he added. 'Quite safe.'

'How do I know? I don't know you.'

'My name's Matthew Craven and I live in Marine Cottage—I'm an artist—and I've been there two months, and I pay my bills regularly, Mrs Patterson in the village store will tell you that. Do I look like a rapist?'

She vaguely remembered her Aunt Peggy mentioning a stranger taking the old cottage by the dunes, and saying she'd passed the time of day with him one morning in the store, and how he'd been ordering paints. She began to laugh, softly at first, then louder, in sheer heartfelt relief.

'I'm sorry. You must think me an awful timid creature, but I don't get out a lot—and I didn't know——'

'How could you?' They were in the trees now, and he walked slightly ahead where they were thicker, pushing the branches out of her way. 'If you never go anywhere? You live with your aunt and uncle, don't you? Don't they like you mixing?' There was no offence in the way he said the words, just a mild curiosity. Yet she felt resentment at them.

'You seem to know a lot about me,' she answered. 'And you're quite wrong. They're kindness itself— you should have found *that* out when you were doing your snooping!'

He stopped walking, turned round, and faced her. 'I didn't "snoop" as you put it. I didn't need to. You're living in a small village. Everyone talks about everyone else, and unless you're deaf you can hardly avoid hearing—and they talk about you simply because you're so aloof——'

'How dare you!' Colour lit her face and she stared at him angrily. 'Who do you think you are to speak to me like that?'

'I've already told you. Are you so prickly with everyone? No wonder they say——'

'I don't want to hear what they say,' she breathed. 'Will you please let me pass?'

'When I'm ready. I've told you you're quite safe, and you are. I've no taste for attacking women—but I don't like being insulted either.'

'Insulted? You're the insulting one, with your questions. I was having a quiet walk, minding my own business, and you come up and start asking me all sorts of things, as though you've the right——'

'Maybe I have.' He turned and walked on, and the words tingled in her ears. As they came out of the trees they saw the house, and she was about to ask him what he had meant when she saw the door standing wide open.

'What? Oh——' She began to walk more quickly, wondering what had happened, and the question went out of her head. She forgot him as she went up to the door. And then she stopped. She had closed it; she was positive she had closed it. What if someone was inside?

'What's the matter?' He had dropped his sack and followed her. She turned to him, and for a split second she was undecided whether to appeal to him or not. Which was worse? Him or someone else—in the house?

He had seen the door, and he frowned. 'I take it it should be closed?'

'Yes.' She bit her lip. She had been going to give the game away, before she thought. 'Only my aunt and uncle have gone out for the day——'

'A day trip—to Canada? What are they in—Concorde?' She should have known he would know that as well. She stared at him, wordless. He smiled gently down at her. 'They've gone on holiday, haven't they?'

'You already know. Why ask?' she answered dully.

'And you're staying here—alone—for three weeks.'

It wasn't a question, it was a statement. She nodded. 'Yes.'

'Then wouldn't you prefer me to look around for you and make sure no one's inside the house?'

She didn't want him inside, she had already made her mind up on that when they had been walking back, but the open door put a different complexion on things. If she went in alone, now, she would not have an easy moment until she had searched the house from top to bottom, not knowing, wondering all the time. . . . 'Please,' she said.

'Come on then. You show me around.' They went in, and he did a strange thing—he bolted the door. Seeing her face, he explained, 'If anyone is in, we'll know, won't we?'

'I suppose so.'

'Now the back door. Lead the way.' She walked

through the hall and he followed, his heavy steps solid and reassuring behind her. She put the chain on the back door and he looked around. 'All right. Now, every room, and we close each door after us. Right?' He opened the door to the pantry, looked inside, and closed it again. Then systematically they went through the entire house from cellars to attics, and looked in every cupboard and wardrobe. Matthew Craven moved swiftly and silently, and Siana followed, and if there had been anyone hiding he would have found them, or heard them, so quietly did he conduct his search—and without a word.

Then at last they were in the large hall again and he looked at her. 'There is no one,' he said. 'And I doubt if anyone's been in, do you?'

'Nothing's been disturbed.' She pushed her hair back from her forehead. 'Thank you, Mr Craven. Can I make you a drink?'

'Are you sure you want to?'

She flushed. 'It's the least I can do.'

'Very well. Thank you, I'll have a coffee if I may.'

She led the way out to the kitchen and he followed. 'Aren't you nervous, being on your own?'

'I wasn't——' She was putting the kettle on as she said the words, and realised they could be misinterpreted. 'I meant——'

'I think I know what you meant,' he said. She turned away again and busied herself with cups, coffee, milk. She knew now what it was about him that disturbed her. It was the way he watched her. It was the way he looked at her, as if his eyes searched for something, and she was uneasy.

He sat down and pulled the morning's paper to him, glancing at the headlines and then at Siana. 'I suppose you have to go in and buy this every day?'

'Yes. They don't deliver out here. Nor milk.'

'Same with me. It's a wonder I've not seen you in the shop.'

'My uncle usually goes. He's retired, he likes the walk.' She handed him the coffee. 'Help yourself to sugar.'

'Thanks. I suppose that's a job you'll have to do for the next three weeks, then?'

'I suppose so. Why do you ask?' She looked at him, wishing he would go away and leave her alone. 'What does it matter to you?' She hadn't intended the words to come out so sharply, but they did.

He lifted an eyebrow, amused. 'I was going to offer to do it for you—to save you a journey, that's all. My house is very near here.'

She felt foolish, but at the same time she resented him. 'Oh, I see. I'll manage, thanks.' Why didn't he drink his coffee and go?

It seemed as if he was a mind-reader as well. He finished drinking and stood up. 'I have jobs to do,' he said, quite pleasantly. 'I suggest you lock your doors next time you go out. While you're alone, that is.'

'Yes, I will.' She had no intention of telling him she hadn't a clue where the keys were. 'And—thank you.'

'A pleasure. I'll see myself out.'

'Oh, but——' she began, but he'd gone. Just walked out, and she heard him going across the hall, his footsteps solid, unbolt the door, then it closed.

Siana sat down very slowly at the table. There had been nothing to take exception to in his behaviour—and yet she felt almost as if she had been assaulted. An odd sensation to have, and she recalled his manner when they had met, the way he had moved, the things he had said—and how he had looked at her. It was this last which caused her more concern than anything. With him steadily watching, his dark eyes shrewd and far-seeing, she had felt stripped of all pretence—as if he knew all about her. Yet how could he? She didn't even know that herself. She touched his still warm cup, and shivered slightly. He was a threat to her, but in what way she did not know. Very slowly she stood up and walked across the hall to bolt the front door.

The nightmare came again that night. The one in which she was in a car that rolled and plunged over a cliff and down, down, down into the bottomless sea, and in the nightmare, always, she could hear herself screaming as loudly as she could—and knowing no one else in the world could hear.

She sat bolt upright, covered in perspiration, and stared at the pale path of moonlight coming in through the undrawn curtains, tracing its silvery pattern across the carpet. She hadn't had the dream for ages, and had hoped it had gone for good. Now she knew it hadn't. There would be no sleep again for her, she was too tense. Slipping on her dressing gown, she went down to the kitchen and brewed a pot of tea, and while she sat at the table drinking it she thought about her visitor, because she didn't want to think about the nightmare. What was there about a reasonably courteous stranger that should frighten her so? Yet she knew. She knew inwardly, and in a way she was not prepared to admit, either to herself or to anyone else. It was quite simply because he was a man—a strong, virile man, probably in mid-thirties, and attractive with that confidence and assurance she herself lacked.

She looked, unseeing, towards the window, the image of him coming strongly to her mind. Gently she smoothed her hair back from her face. It would be better if she did not see him again, but she knew she couldn't avoid it. She was going to.

It was nearly seven. Already the sky was paling with the distant approach of dawn, and from somewhere far away a bird called; a single note, to be followed by others. She went and opened the back door and stood on the step, listening. The memory of the nightmare was fading, and already it seemed unreal, no longer as frightening—then she heard him call her name.

'Siana!' At first, for a moment, she thought she had imagined it, and she caught her breath—then he appeared, walking soft-footed from out of the trees, and it was no imagination, it was the man.

'Are you all right? I saw the light go on.'

She wanted to rush in and slam the door, but

something stopped her. 'What are you doing here?' she asked.

'I often get up early and go out fishing.' He was there in front of her now, clad in the same clothes as the previous day, and he had a basket slung on canvas from his left shoulder. 'Fancy some fish for breakfast?'

'No, thanks. I heard a noise and came down——' It was a stupid thing to say, but for the moment she couldn't think of anything else, only that there was no way she could tell him or anyone else about the dream.

He came up the steps. 'A noise?' he frowned. 'And you came down and stood at the *door*?'

Siana knew she shouldn't have said it. It was practically issuing an invitation for him to come in. 'Only—only like an animal——' she lied, and faltered in the words. He knew she was lying, just as if she had told him.

'I've heard nothing.'

'Then it must have been my imagination. I'll go back to bed now——' she half turned in dismissal, and he said softly:

'I've told you, you needn't be scared of me.'

'What makes you think I am?'

'Everything about you. The way you talk, the way you look at me——'

'Then why don't you have the decency to go?'

'I don't give up so easily.'

'What do you mean?' She stared at him in alarm.

'Don't you know?' There was something in the way he said the words that was more frightening than any nightmare. Then he smiled. Dear God, she thought, he's insane. He's a madman, and I'm standing here talking to him, and any minute now he'll come in and there's nothing I can do to stop him. She clutched at the door, and if she had had the strength to slam it in his face she would have done, but he was too close. He only had to reach out his hand to stop her.

'Please—please, go away,' she whispered.

'I want to talk to you first. That's all—to talk.'

'There's nothing to say.'

'There's a lot to say. I think I can help you.'

'Help me?' she croaked. 'Help *me*?' She wanted to laugh, but couldn't.

'Yes. To get your memory back.'

She thought she was going to faint. Dark waves came rushing into her head, filling her senses, drowning her—then he caught her by the arms and said gently: 'It's all right, I know all about it.'

'But—how—how——' He led her over to a chair and pushed her gently into it.

'Don't try and say anything yet,' he cautioned. 'Just sit quietly. May I make some tea?'

'Yes.' She began to shiver. The morning was cold and the central heating was as yet low in the kitchen. Matthew Craven took off his jacket and draped it over her shoulders.

'Put that on, it's warm.'

'But—you'll be cold——'

'I never feel the cold. Certainly not in here.' He looked at the fireplace. 'Shall I light a fire?'

'No, I'll put this on, thanks.' She didn't want to,

it was too personal somehow, but there seemed no way to refuse, and she didn't feel strong enough. The jacket, a thick dark blue anorak, was too large, but it was immediately warming, as though from his body heat. It smelt faintly of tobacco, and salty sea air. Siana watched him fill the kettle and put it on, saw how big and broad-shouldered he was, how deft and economical his movements, and it all seemed to threaten her, as if he were taking over. His words had had an odd effect on her. He knew too much, and she didn't want him to know anything. She wanted him to go away.

'Here you are. Sugar?'

'No, thanks.' She took the beakerful from him and cupped her hands round it, seeking more warmth and perhaps some reassurance that the world was still normal.

'I'm going to cook you some fish for breakfast,' he said, and as she opened her mouth to protest, he added: 'You don't eat enough.'

'What do you mean?' she burst out indignantly. 'I eat well——'

'You're too thin for your height——'

'And you're very personal! I'm quite capable of making my own breakfast, thank you——'

'And what will that be? A piece of toast?' He was busily sorting through his basket of fish as he spoke, and he wasn't looking at her, his back was to her and she had the sudden helpless feeling that he was just going to stay, and take over, and there seemed nothing she would be able to do about it,

that was the awful thing. She felt frightened,
stifled, but she had spirit enough to retort:

'I'll have some porridge——'

'Porridge? You can have that later. Where's your
frying pan? Just show me where everything is, then
go and get dressed.'

She stood up. 'No. I want you to leave.'

He turned round then, and looked at her. 'Before you know what I've got to say? I don't think
you do. Do I scare you so?'

Her eyes told him, and she saw a muscle move in
his jaw, heard the soft hiss of his indrawn breath.
'No,' he said softly, 'I'm not a madman, I promise
you.' He must have read her thoughts, and that was
even more frightening. 'And you're in no danger
from me.'

'Can you blame me——' she began.

He shook his head gently. 'No,' he said. 'No, I
don't. But you need looking after. Is it so wrong of
me to offer to make your breakfast? Are you so cut
off from the world that you resent any intrusion
into your life?'

'Does it matter? Does it have anything to do with
you?' she demanded.

'You're a fellow human being. A woman, a vulnerable woman——'

'No! You don't know me——' she burst out.

'I know a lot about you. More than you think.'
He began to open cupboards. 'May I?' It was a
rhetorical question. 'Ah, here they are.' He began
to lift out pans and plates. 'I listen when people

talk. I listen, and observe, and keep quiet—that way I find out.'

'There's not much to find out——'

'There is. And I have. I know, for a start, that you were brought here by your aunt and uncle two years ago after being in a car crash, and after leaving hospital with no memory of your life before. I know that they'd lost touch with you five years before that, that they recognised your photo in the newspaper when police appealed for someone to identify you—and that you've remembered nothing since then. Your life during those five missing years is still a blank——'

'I think,' she said breathlessly, 'that you've said enough.'

'But what I say is true, isn't it?'

'If it is? What then? You can't help.' He ignored her. He was busy filleting the fish at the sink, and had his back to her, so that she couldn't see his face.

'Cooking oil?' he said, as if she hadn't spoken at all. 'Just a drop.' She got up from the table, because it was easier than sitting there waiting with that odd feeling of helplessness for whatever he might choose to say.

'Here.' She handed him the bottle. 'You didn't answer me.'

'No. After we've eaten.' And he grinned at her. It certainly changed his face. For a moment he didn't seem sinister at all.

'Do you always invite yourself to breakfast with people you don't know?' she asked, breathless.

'First time I've tried it. This kitchen is certainly

a lot bigger than mine. And much more modern. Very nice.'

'Damn your kitchen!' she burst out. 'I want you to go away!'

'No, you don't. You think you do, because you've been conditioned to reject people——'

'How dare you!' Siana was incensed, the more so because he was making it difficult for her by being so busy at the cooker, as though she was merely discussing the weather, nothing of any importance at all. 'Please have the manners to look at me when I'm talking to you!'

He turned smartly. 'Yes, ma'am.' The fish was in the pan, beginning to sizzle gently. 'What is it?'

'What do you mean I've been conditioned——'

'Because of your lost memory. Your aunt and uncle protect you too much——'

'That's absurd!'

'Is it? Absurd? Then who refused all social invitations? You?'

'I don't know what you mean.' She was puzzled. Social invitations? Where did he think he was—London?

'The village socials. There was one a few weeks ago, in the village hall. I was there, everyone was—you weren't, nor your aunt and uncle——'

'Just because I don't want to go out—I can't dance—or hadn't you noticed my leg? Don't tell me you were too polite to comment on the fact that I limp? You're insensitive enough about everything else——'

'Did you *know* about the social?'

She could lie. She could say, of course I did—but instead she shook her head. 'No. They—my uncle's very forgetful——'

'All the time? Like the cinema show last week? Did they forget that too?' She was silenced. 'He told them you were ill last week. Were you?'

She looked at him. 'I—I don't believe you.' But it showed in her eyes. And she remembered the frequent occasions she had entered a room and seen an exchanged glance, words hastily altered, and wondered.

'You can check, if you need to,' he said softly. 'But I don't think you do.'

'It's because—if they do, it's because they worry about me,' she retorted, on the defensive now. 'They took me in, they look after me—and anyway, if they were so possessive, as *you* say, why would they have gone to Canada and left me alone?'

'Perhaps they had no choice,' he said flatly.

Siana suddenly found herself beginning to shiver. It was as though a chill had entered the room. And Matthew Craven had brought it. He had put doubt in her mind. Something had changed, and would never be the same again.

She sat down at the table and clutched his jacket around her, unaware that she was doing so, heedless of the fact that she still had her night clothes on. He turned and looked at her, and said more gently: 'The fish is nearly ready. You'll feel better after you've eaten.'

'I'm not hungry.'

'You will be in a moment. I'm a good cook.'

She stared into space as he buttered bread and put it on the table, then placed a plate in front of her. 'Eat,' he said.

Siana began to eat, because it seemed easier than trying to argue. Of course there would be a perfectly rational explanation for everything. She only had to ask Aunt Peggy when she telephoned, and she would make it all right again. She had already called the previous evening to say they had arrived safely, and was going to telephone every evening about nine. Siana hadn't told her about her encounter with Matthew Craven, because she hadn't wanted to worry her aunt.

'Does it taste okay?' his voice broke into her thoughts.

'Oh—er—yes. Thank you.'

'After we've eaten I'll go. That is what you want, isn't it?' He looked at her across the table, and the expression in his eyes was unreadable, dark, mysterious—like him.

'Yes. I'm sorry, I'm afraid I do.'

'That's all right,' he said cheerfully. 'I can take a hint. And you've given enough. I'd like a cup of coffee before I go. Would you?'

'Yes. I'll make it.' She had finished the fish, much to her surprise, and it had been delicious. She took her plate to the sink, and filled the kettle. Something was disturbing her, but she couldn't think what it was. Merely an elusive thought at the back of her mind that was unformed, but refused to go away. There was also a mingling of relief that she would soon be rid of him. With any luck, she might not see him again. ...

He was behind her, too close, not touching, but intruding on the space she liked to keep round herself, and she moved slightly aside, and he put his plate in the sink, and said:

'I'll get milk and papers for you if you like. I'm going to the shops now.'

'No, thanks, I'll manage.'

'Fine.' Siana poured the coffee out and he took his and sat down. And now he didn't speak. He looked at her, but he didn't say anything.

'You said you're an artist?' She couldn't bear the silence any longer.

'Well,' he managed to look almost modest, 'that was a slight exaggeration. I paint—let's put it that way.'

'You earn a living from it?'

'Not exactly. But I manage.'

She didn't want to know anything about him, because he was too disturbing, and he made her uneasy, and she didn't like it and she didn't like him, but she couldn't bear the silence, and him just looking at her as though he knew everything about her. 'Do you sell any?'

'A few. Not here, of course. Mainly in Edinburgh.'

'Oh, you come from there?'

'Do I sound Scottish? No. But I have friends there.'

'You've taken Marine Cottage, you said. For long?'

'You mean when will I be moving away?' She felt herself go pink at the accuracy of his question. 'Not yet. I have things to do first.' His grey eyes were very steady on her, and it was as if they looked into her very being. She turned away. She hadn't sat down again with her coffee, she had remained standing deliberately so that he might leave more quickly. She finished her coffee and began to run the tap for hot water to wash the dishes, and he handed her his empty cup, and said: 'Thanks for the breakfast.'

'Thank you for the fish. I enjoyed it.' He was going. She could afford to be generous.

'Good. Shall I leave you a couple for your supper?'

'Only if you can spare them.'

'I can.' He lifted two out of the basket and put them on a clean plate. 'Er—may I have my jacket?'

'Sorry.' She took it off. He put it on, then shouldered the basket.

'Well, I'm off.' He opened the back door, and she followed him—to make sure she bolted it after him. If he came again she would pretend to be out.

He looked up at the sky. 'Looks like we'll have snow later.' He smiled at her. 'Keep warm.'

'I will. Goodbye.'

She watched him striding out across the back garden towards the trees, and bolted the door. He had gone, he had actually gone. She made herself another cup of coffee to celebrate, sat down at the table, and began to drink it. She could relax now. She didn't have to see him again, nor would she have to listen to his disturbing words. He had really gone.

It was only much later that she found the wallet under the kitchen table as she tidied up. She looked at it in something approaching horror, then bent to pick it up.

CHAPTER TWO

THE wallet was old and battered-looking, and as it certainly didn't belong to either Uncle Peter or her aunt, there was only one person it could belong to. Siana left it on the table while she thought about what to do. The threatened snow was already coming down, had covered the grass with a fine silver dust that was as yet hardly measurable, but it looked as though it had set in for the day.

There was only one thing to do, and that was to return it to Marine Cottage herself. If she didn't, the inevitable would happen: Matthew Craven would be back. And she didn't want that, not under any circumstances.

Siana stood at the window and watched the flakes falling with increased speed and thickness. 'Damn, damn,' she muttered. Why did it have to snow now of all times? She was always nervous of slipping in snow, and generally avoided going out in it. She had already been to the village store for milk, groceries, and daily papers, and there would have been no need for her to leave the house again that day. There was plenty of housework to keep her busy, and several good books she would now have time to read, being alone, and this had to happen. She glared at the wallet in exasperation. It must have fallen out of his jacket when he put it round her. Suppose he was looking for it now? Suppose he was on his way to the house? Suppose....

It was no use standing there. The snow wouldn't vanish for wishing about it, and conditions certainly wouldn't improve, would get far worse when it began to go dark in an hour or so. Siana picked it up and held it. The temptation to open it was irresistible, but she fought it. If she had found it outside, obviously she would have needed to see who it belonged to, but she already knew that. She put it down again and went to get her coat and wellingtons.

Five minutes later, snugly clad against the cold late afternoon air, she set off from the house, leaving two lights on—why, she didn't know, except that she had no key and couldn't lock the door, and it seemed more welcoming to return to. The sky was heavy with snow, darkening rapidly, and the air was cold so that her breath became steam, and her coat was fluffy white with clinging snowflakes. The wallet was in her pocket.

There was a path through the trees, which led eventually to the village, and once among the trees there was no snow, but it was darker. Siana felt no fear of being alone; there was an atmosphere of peace and calm, surrounded by the tall dark trees, and no sounds at all, save the distant one of the sea. She would soon be there, another three minutes and the trees would end, and she would see his house. She had passed it often when it had been empty, had once looked in the windows at the dusty rooms with their old furniture and faded wallpaper. It was only small, a whitewashed two-bedroomed cottage, but it had character and charm, and was very old. Siana had sometimes wondered what it would be like to live there on her own, to come and go as and when she pleased, and keep a cat and a dog, and perhaps a few hens. She had never mentioned this harmless fantasy to her aunt and uncle; they wouldn't have understood. She loved them, and felt secure with them, but Matthew Craven had been very near the mark with some of his comments, although she wouldn't for the world admit it. She occasionally felt stifled at Craig House, yet in no way she could put her finger on. It was as if they wished to cocoon her from the harsh world. Perhaps, she thought, as she neared the cottage, they've succeeded.

The house was in darkness. Smoke rose from the chimney, and the snowflakes whirled around her face, blinding her for a few moments. She brushed the snow from her eyes and knocked at the door. She would hand it to him, and go. Silence; no footsteps, nothing. She knocked again, and the knocks echoed through the cottage, and she knew it was empty. For one ridiculous moment she wasn't sure if she felt relieved—or dismayed.

Lifting the flap of the letter box, Siana pushed the wallet through and heard it fall to the floor. Then, turning, she set off back towards home.

That was done—perfect, really. She hadn't had to see him again. The snow was really thick now, the flakes heavy and clinging and cold, stinging her cheeks and nose. She put out her tongue and tasted one, and laughed at herself for being so childish. Then she was in the trees, and it was really quite dark, after the blurred dazzle of the whiteness; she walked quicker, promising herself a cup of tea when she got in, and a warm fire in the kitchen, and a good read. . . .

The crackling warned her first, the crunching of twigs underfoot, ahead of her, and she paused to listen, to make sure—then a tall figure loomed out of the darkness and came nearer; she stood still, poised for flight, and he said: 'Siana?' it was Matthew Craven. He came nearer, and he too was covered in snow, his jacket and hair white with it, and he laughed. 'I don't believe it! Don't tell me you've just been to my house?'

'Yes. I found your wallet——'

'I know. I've just been knocking at your door, but the house was in darkness so I guessed you'd gone to the village—or Marine Cottage.'

'I didn't see you on my way there,' she said, not realising yet what he had said.

'No, because I didn't go directly. I went for a walk on the beach and took the long way round. I should have gone straight there, it would have saved you a journey.'

'Well, it's done now. I posted it through your letter box—you'll find it safely, I hope. It must have dropped out of your pocket——' then suddenly what he had said registered. 'What do you mean, my house was in darkness? I left the kitchen and hall light on.' She looked at him accusingly, and he smiled.

'You're mistaken. Perhaps you meant to——'

'No, I know I did.' She began walking again, past him. 'I'd better go.'

'Wait, I'll walk with you.'

'There's no need,' she began, and he said softly:

'And if your door is open as well?' Siana stopped, froze, looked at him.

'What do you mean?' She felt stifled.

'I tried your back door—it was unlocked. You're very careless, you know, Siana—and no, before you ask, I didn't go in, I just waited and shouted you. Now, hadn't I better walk you back?' He fell into step beside her and added: 'Don't you have a key?'

She didn't want to tell him. She wanted him to go away. 'Haven't you?' he repeated.

'It's lost. I don't know where it is. People don't need keys around here.'

He made a small, exasperated sound. 'Anyone as jumpy as you does——' he stopped, because they had reached the end of the trees, and they could see the house, and it was in darkness. Siana felt an irrational sense of total fear. She *knew* she had left those lights on, whatever he said.

'Oh, no!' she murmured, shaken.

'Don't say it. I'll come in and check. Okay?'

'I——' she fought silently inside herself, then: 'Please, if you would.'

He opened the kitchen door and the warm air rushed out to meet them, then they were inside the now shadowy kitchen, and Siana went over to the light switch and flicked it on and off. The light stayed off.

'It must be the fuse,' she said.

'And the hall one? Is that on the same fuse?'

'I don't know. I'll try it.' She went out, into the hall, and tried that one. Nothing happened. She tried all the downstairs lights, and none were working. She went back into the kitchen and told him so.

'I'll check all the fuses. Have you a torch?'

'Yes.' She found it in a cupboard and handed it to him. 'In the cellar. This way.'

He locked the back door, and this time she knew why, and didn't ask. He went first down the steep cellar steps and found the fuse boxes and she stood waiting, watching, while he examined them all. Then he turned to her. 'I'm no expert, but they seem all right to me. How is your electricity supplied? From the mains?'

'No. They don't come out this far from the village. We've a dynamo in an outbuilding outside—but it can't be that, my uncle keeps it well maintained——'

'It's something, and I don't think it's your fuses. I'd better have a look.' She led him through the kitchen, out of the back door, and round the side of the house to the small built-on room that housed the dynamo. She knew, before she opened the door, that something was wrong. There was no hum of the motor, just a deadly silence. He went in and she waited in the doorway, and she began to shiver with cold and fear.

She saw the beam of the torch flickering over the silent dynamo, and the water from the hill stream that powered it was still gushing in—but the dynamo remained still and useless. Matthew Craven turned to her, his face a blur in the dim light. 'I'm sorry,' he said, 'but it's certainly not working.'

'What will I do?'

'First, we'll get back into the house. It's too damned cold out here and I can't see anything anyway in this light—and you look half starved.' She stumbled going into the kitchen, and he caught her and stopped her falling. 'Sit down,' he ordered, not ungently. 'I'll make tea. Thank God your cooker is gas.'

'But the dynamo works the central heating as well,' she said.

'Does it now? Too bad.' He didn't seem to care, either way. 'You've got fireplaces, haven't you?'

'Yes, but——'

'Any coal?'

'Yes——'

'Well then, you'll have to light a few fires, won't you? I haven't got central heating, and I manage. I haven't got electricity, come to that, only paraffin lamps. You'll live.'

'Thanks. You make me feel much better.'

He looked sharply at her, and even in the gloom she saw his expression. 'Don't tell me you feel sorry for yourself? I thought you were totally independent.'

Siana lifted her chin. 'I am.'

'Fine. Where's the milk? It's not in the fridge.'

'Oh, on the windowsill.' She went to fetch it, handed him a bottle. The dread was growing, but she wasn't going to show it. The house would be in darkness, and growing colder each minute as the heating died down. 'I'll light a fire,' she told him.

'Got any paraffin lamps?'

'Er—no.'

'My God! Aren't you prepared for emergencies?'

'My uncle's always here,' she retorted defensively.

'He's not now, is he? He's in Canada. That's not much help.'

'I'll manage,' she gritted.

'Like hell you will. That torch will last a few hours—it's Sunday tomorrow, it's snowing like it means it—you could be snowed up without food or light and you say you'll manage. Hah!'

'Oh, shut up!' she burst out. 'Why don't you trot off back to your cosy little cottage and sit there smugly by your paraffin lamp and just think how clever you are——'

'And losing your temper won't get you far either. It wastes energy. Better get some firelighters—I suppose you *do* have those?'

'I'll make some with newspaper,' she said with dignity.

'Drink your tea first. Then sit down, make your firelighters, and I'll go home and bring back a spare lamp for you, okay?'

Temptation rose, was squashed. Meekly, Siana said: 'Thank you. It's very kind of you.'

'I know,' he answered smoothly. 'I thought for a moment you were going to tell me what to do with my lamp—but you're learning.'

She took a deep breath. The man was insufferable! Smug wasn't the right word. Bossy was more like it. And there was nothing she could do about it, so she drank her tea.

When Matthew Craven had finished his, he said: 'I'm off now. Get your paper spills made—I'll see you soon.' Then he went out, leaving a brief flurry of snowflakes whirling in before he shut the door.

She remembered, after he'd gone, and all was silent, that they hadn't checked round the house. She sat very still. The reason the lights had gone out was simply because of the dynamo, not intruders, but——

She seemed to hear little noises, small creakings from somewhere, vague amorphous sounds, nothing tangible, as if someone was waiting. . . .

Siana stood up and faced the door to the hall. 'Don't be *stupid*,' she said fiercely out loud. But not for anything would she have opened that door. How long would he be? She pictured him walking through the trees. He'd soon be at his cottage, she could almost time him. She went to the window to see a blinding whiteness, a blur of snowflakes, clinging to the window before melting and fading, then more, and more, millions of them. The kitchen was growing colder, unless it was her imagination— she shivered, and she couldn't remember where the newspapers were. She couldn't think of anything except that she was suddenly frightened, and she wished Matthew Craven would return. She had never thought she would be glad to see him.

She switched on two gas rings, and the warmth was instant, and comforting. She stood by the cooker and smelt the faint but unmistakable scent of Calor gas. At least there was plenty of that. Or was there? How could she be sure? She switched on the torch and looked at the container beside the cooker as if it might tell her. Uncle Peter had four cylinders delivered at a time, and they were due again next week....

She turned the gas off. Better not to chance it, not now. Fifteen minutes had passed; he should be back any time. She stood by the window, not seeing anything, only whiteness that was becoming sinister. Suppose he reached his house and couldn't make it back? Suppose he'd decided it was too bad to set out, and would wait a while? Suppose—— 'No, stop it,' she whispered. 'Stop it. He'll be back——'

But the minutes passed, ticked inexorably by, and there was nothing, only the blinding white silence, and the waiting. Waiting. Siana went to the door and wrenched it open, and saw the snow piling on the step, inches deep already and growing. Half an hour had passed; he'd had time to make the journey twice. She tried to calm herself, but in vain. If he wasn't here in another five minutes she would put her coat and boots on and go because one thing was certain, she couldn't stay in the house any longer, not alone, not with those noises, the creaks and rustlings——

She began to put her coat on in readiness, slipping the wellingtons she had taken off on entering on again, and stood by the window. She could make it to his cottage, but not the village, she knew that.

And suppose, when she reached it, he wasn't there? She fought down panic. It had been so nice, the thought of being on her own for three weeks, just to do as she pleased, when she pleased, feeling free.... But this wasn't freedom, it was nightmare. And Matthew Craven had changed from unwelcome intruder to someone solid and dependable. Bossy, yes—but not frightened of anything, not a shivering, quaking coward like me, she thought. She put her hand to her mouth and pressed it hard. That's what I am, I know it now. They're right, my aunt and uncle, I'm not grown up. I'm not capable of running my own life. Perhaps that's why they went, to show me just how badly I'd cope on my own— only they couldn't have planned this weather, they couldn't have known about this, and the dynamo—

She began to tremble violently, helplessly—then the door swung open, and Matthew Craven staggered in, heavily laden, and said: 'Bloody hell!' and she rushed towards him and flung her arms round him, snow and all, and said:

'Oh. Oh! *Thank* you!'

He began to laugh, held her away from him, looked down at her, and said: 'You'll get soaked! That was a nice welcome—but I don't want you getting pneumonia. Why the coat?'

'I was going to set out——' she began, teeth chattering. The smile vanished, and he looked at her soberly.

'You were? You really were? Why?'

'I thought—you wouldn't come back. I—the

house—I heard sounds——' She looked at him, hardly seeing anything, only the vague snow-covered shadowy blur that he was, but her heart thudded in sheer relief. She had never been so glad to see anyone in her life.

He shook his head. 'There's no one here. I'll check once we've got some light going.' She saw then that he had a large duffel bag slung over his shoulder. He put it gently to the floor, opened it, and took out a lamp. 'I've brought spare paraffin as well. Let me get this going.'

He took off his coat and she carried it to the door, opened it and shook it quickly outside before slamming and bolting the door. She was nearly crying with the release from tension. 'I'll make you a hot drink while you light the lamp,' she said. 'Tea or coffee?'

'Coffee, please.' He was fiddling with the wick, then light glowed and flooded the room, and he put back the glass shade. 'How's that?'

'Lovely.' It was too. To be able to actually see, and to feel the tension and fear ebbing away as fast as melting snow, made her almost lightheaded with relief. 'I couldn't remember where the newspapers were to start the fire——'

'Or you were too scared to look?'

'Yes,' she admitted.

'I've brought some food. I didn't know if you have much in——'

'Oh yes. A pantryful of tinned stuff and potatoes and oats——'

'That's a relief. You do realise that by tomorrow it'll be impossible to move, don't you?'

'Is it—is it that bad?' she asked faintly.

'It is. That's why I've brought some clothes as well. I'm staying here with you, Siana.' His words had more of a shock effect because they were so casually said. For a moment she was literally speechless, and he continued softly: 'You do realise that you couldn't manage alone, don't you?'

That was what Aunty Peggy and Uncle Peter were always saying, and somehow hearing the same words from him was so much worse. The sense of relief ebbed away and she stared at him, dazed.

'No. Oh—no——' she began.

'Because of the conventions? Because I'm a stranger?' he said harshly. 'Do you think I intend to harm you?'

She sat down, leaving the kettle to boil unheeded, until he switched it off. 'Do you?' he repeated.

She hadn't imagined this. She hadn't visualised anything further than his return with the lamp. She looked up at him helplessly. 'Hadn't you better make that coffee?' he said. 'You've been scared of me ever since I spoke to you on the beach, haven't you? Admit it.' His face was hard and dark, shadowed away from the light, and Siana's irrational fears swept back, filling her. 'Why are you so frightened? Is it me—or men in general? You didn't seem scared when you greeted me at the door. In fact I'd have said you were pleased to see me.' He stopped. Then as she neither moved nor spoke he came over and pulled her to her feet, and shook her.

'My God, what is it with you?'

'I don't—know.'

'You're trembling. Is that what I do to you? Answer me!'

Siana swallowed. 'Please let me go.'

He released her so suddenly that she nearly fell, and she clutched at the table for support. He turned away as if tired of talking and went over to the cooker. 'What have they done? Brainwashed you into believing all men are beasts?' He turned to her again.

'Of course not—that's ridic——'

'I'm not so sure it's ridiculous at all. Something's made you act like a terrified virgin——'

'How dare you! You don't understand——'

'But I'm beginning to. You're glad enough of help when you need it. Just as long as it's only as much as you want to accept. Think, Siana—if I went now. Think about it. You're scared of noises in the house—would you search it—alone? Would you?' She shook her head. 'And if the lamp went out, would you know how to trim it and light it?' He didn't give her a chance to answer. He went on, inexorably: 'What would you do if the water pipes freeze? And your gas tank's nearly empty, I noticed that before. Have you another cylinder? And would you know how to attach it if you had?' She sat down and put her hands over her ears to stop his dreadful words, but he strode over and took them away. 'The answer's no to everything. And you think you can manage. My God, it's like leaving a child alone in a house! You're——'

Siana hit him with all her strength, hard on his face. Then, sobbing, she ran out of the kitchen.

CHAPTER THREE

SIANA stumbled up the stairs in pitch blackness, and into her bedroom. There she sat on her bed and hugged her arms round her, shaking and shivering. The awful thing was that all his words were dreadfully true. He had also said she was like a child. Perhaps he was as right in that as in everything else. She gazed blankly into the darkness, relieved only by the whitish blur outside. How would she cope alone? Perhaps, if the dynamo hadn't broken down, she would have managed. But not without electricity. And there was nowhere to run to, no shelter she could seek. Her only shelter lay here—with him. She went over to the window, and now the house seemed as though it were a prison, a white snowbound prison, with a jailer who thought of her with contempt. She closed her eyes and prayed for strength. Gradually she became calmer, and she knew she had to go downstairs and face him. She took a deep breath. The longer she postponed it the more difficult it would be. She had struck him in anger and fear, and now she regretted it. As she walked slowly down the stairs in the dark, breathing deeply to calm herself, she came to a decision: she had no choice. Matthew Craven was going to stay, he had made that quite clear. And in a way, a part of her knew that it was logical and sensible. She would accept it and make the best of the situation: she had to.

She went into the kitchen, and he was lighting a fire with wood and paper. He looked up. 'I'm sorry I hit you,' she said.

'Try not to make a habit of it.' His tone was dry. 'Where else do you want a fire lit? And where do you keep the coal? Outside?'

'No. Past the pantry there's a coalhouse. There's peat as well. Uncle gets that from a villager.'

'I don't know much about peat—although I'm sure I will before I leave.' He smiled slightly, as if he meant he'd be staying quite a while, but Siana knew she must stop reading things into his words or she would go mad, so she said:

'I'll get the coal,' and went out. Only she couldn't see a thing, and had to go back for the torch: Matthew was just drawing the fire with the shovel and paper, and he said:

'Don't take too long.'

Ten minutes later a good blaze was crackling up the chimney, and the kitchen immediately began to feel warmer. 'Now food,' he said. 'Then you can show me where I'm to sleep.'

'What about the cooker?'

'What about it? If the gas runs out we'll start cooking on the fire. Until then, we'll use it.' And that was that, she thought. He didn't dither about, as Siana knew she would have done, wondering whether she dared use any precious gas. He made it sound so clear cut, and simple.

'Do you have a portable radio—running off a battery, I mean?'

'No—only a plug in one.'

'Damn! I'd better go and get mine. We'll need the news to see how bad—and how widespread— this snow is. I'll get the other fish as well. Let's sit down and think before I go. Is there anything you can think of that I have that we might need? After tonight I may not be able to go.'

She looked at him, and he sat down at the table. 'Sit down,' he said. 'Well?'

'No.' She sat opposite him. 'There's plenty of food—enough for weeks—and coal, and news-papers.' She paused, casting a mental eye over the house and its contents, and he said quietly:

'Good, keep thinking constructively. Main items are always food—heat—light: the necessities. Any-thing else is a bonus. Food's okay, coal the same. I'll try and bring more paraffin, and a torch. But we'll just have to be careful to use it only when we start stumbling about. The radio's not top priority, but it's nice to keep in touch with the outside world——'

'There's the telephone,' she began.

'For how long? We don't know. If your aunt rings tell her about the snow and not to worry if she can't get through again. Are you going to tell her about me?'

The question, coming hard on the heels of prac-ticalities, took her by surprise—as it was doubtless intended to, she realised a moment later.

'I—no,' she said.

A muscle twitched at the corner of his mouth. Not a smile, just a glimmer of one. 'Very wise,' he said drily.

Siana took a deep breath. 'It's not for the reasons you think——'

'What reasons do *I* think?' he interrupted.

'She—you think she'd be angry——' she began, confused, 'but it's not that. It's——' she stopped, unable to put it into words.

'It's what?' he asked, softly, very softly.

'I don't know.' She shook her head, obscurely angry with him, with her aunt, with herself. 'Leave it.'

'No, you must be certain of what you say. She'll guess, if there's anything in your voice—she'll sense it, and worry.'

'Wouldn't you?' she asked bitterly, 'if you'd left your niece alone and found a man had moved in the moment you'd gone?'

'You make it sound as though we're lovers. This is an emergency situation, or hadn't you noticed?'

Lovers, he said. She closed her eyes, suddenly dizzy with the strangest sensation, almost of floating. Lovers. The very word had a mystery about it.

'It's all right. We're not,' he said softly. 'Are we?'

She stood up. 'Hadn't you better go now?' Her heart was pounding.

'I'm going.' He took clothing out of the duffel bag and put it on a chair. 'But think well what you'll say. Reassure her that you're safe and warm and have plenty of food—I wouldn't mention the lack of electricity if I were you.'

'No, of course not.' All was normal again. The moment had passed. Matthew hadn't meant anything by those words. She was too touchy, too sensitive, ready to shy at the slightest thing. 'Can I come with you?'

He looked at her. 'Don't you want to be alone?' She shook her head. 'You're not frightened, are you?'

'No.' She wasn't sure any more what she was.

'I'll travel faster alone. The last time was nearly impossible—this will be a struggle——'

'Then don't go. Please—don't go.'

He smiled. 'You've changed your attitude a bit, haven't you?'

'Yes.'

'Are you worried I won't make it? That I'll fall in the snow and lie there, quietly freezing to death——'

'Stop it!' she exclaimed.

'My God! I believe you are.' He came over and gripped her arms tightly. 'Listen, Siana, just listen carefully. Nothing will happen. I'll go and return as quickly as I can, but I must go alone. What time is it now?'

She looked at her watch. 'Nearly seven.'

'Then have a hot meal ready for me at seventhirty precisely, and I'll be sitting at the table to eat it, I promise. Do you understand?'

'Yes,' she whispered.

'Good. I'm going to get my coat on and go. Start cooking, and make it something good and hot. And wipe that anguished expression off your face and think of how you didn't want me here at all——'

She pulled herself free and turned away, but he caught hold of her again and turned her to face him. His eyes were deep and dark as they looked into hers, and for a few moments time stood still and it seemed as if she had known this would happen, and she knew that he was going to kiss her. But he didn't. The thread of tension stretching between them tautened and snapped, and he said; 'I'll be back,' then took his hands away from her arms. Siana stood very still, waiting for she knew not what, unable to move. The next moment she was alone.

There was something rather odd about the telephone call, but it wasn't until it was over, and Siana was able to think about it, that she realised what it was. It was seven-fifteen precisely when it shrilled in the hall, and Siana picked up the torch, turned the gas down under the pans, and went to answer it.

It was Aunty Peggy, and she had heard on the news that Scotland had been blanketed by snow and was calling early to find out how Siana was. 'I'm fine,' Siana told her. 'The snow is thick, but there's loads of food so I won't need to go out. Don't worry if you're not able to get through any time though. It'll only be the snow cutting the phones off.'

'And you'll stay in, dear?' Her aunt's voice came

over clearly across the thousands of miles separating them. 'I was so worried when I heard the news——'

'Please, you mustn't be. I'm snug and warm and I've plenty to do in the house.'

'That's a relief. You promise you won't venture out?'

'I promise.'

'Only with your leg, you know, I'd worry. You'd better give Mrs Patterson a quick call and tell her you're safe, then she won't be sending anyone——'

'That's a good idea. I will. I'll do it right away.'

'Only with you going in for milk and papers—did you go today?'

'Yes. Before the snow began, only we didn't know then——'

'Of course. Well, that's a relief, knowing you're all right I mean, and you won't need to go out for anything. Don't forget to take your pills. I'll try and call you tomorrow. Uncle Peter sends his love. 'Bye, darling.'

'I won't forget. 'Bye. Give him my love too.' The line clicked, and went dead.

Siana dialled the number of the village store and told Mrs Patterson that although, obviously, she wouldn't be calling in for a few days, she was fine, in case anyone was worried. That task done, she returned to the kitchen and thought about why she should feel slightly puzzled over her aunt's concern.

It came to her as she waited by the window for Matthew to return. He had promised to be back

at seven-thirty, and if he was to keep his promise
he should appear within five minutes. They hadn't
wanted her to go to the village at all while they
were away. Her uncle had bought in a dozen tins
of powdered milk and remarked jokingly that it
would save her the long walk to the shop, and Aunt
Peggy had seemed to think it was a good idea too,
and looked at him in a certain way when Siana had
assured them she loved a walk. And when she
thought about it, how many times had she ever
been to the village in the past two years? A handful
only, and only once alone, because Uncle Peter had
always accompanied her. She had never thought
anything of it. She did now. The one unavoidable
time was when they had both been ill with 'flu,
and she'd had no time to stay and talk then, because of the guilty feeling that she didn't want to
leave them alone.

That had been relief in Aunt Peggy's voice when
she knew Siana wouldn't be going out. Siana
frowned, worried and puzzled. More memories
came flooding back. A few weeks ago she had mentioned the stranger she'd seen in the distance on
the beach—she hadn't known it was Matthew
then—and had seen the look exchanged by her
aunt and uncle before Aunt Peggy had told her
who he was. And in her words, although there had
been nothing tangible, had been the seeds of doubt
sown. A painter, she had said, and yes, she'd seen
him in the village store—again the look at Uncle
Peter—and Siana couldn't yet remember the exact

words, but the implications that had lingered had been that he was obviously a doubtful character, best avoided....

She stared out of the window, knowing now why she had been uneasy when Matthew first spoke to her. The uneasiness had been caused by Aunty Peggy's words. The question now to be answered was: Why? Why did they not want her to get to know people? Why had they turned down all invitations—without even letting her know of them? She knew Matthew had spoken the truth on that. She knew instinctively, but because it seemed too absurd she had denied it. There was no sense in doing so any longer. She was alone, at least for a few minutes, and could think clearly about it. He had said they were over-protective, or words to that effect. It was understandable, Siana supposed. A childless, middle-aged couple leading a quiet life, obviously very fond of her—she stopped. But are they? she thought. Are they really fond of me? She began to feel quite suddenly as if she were terribly alone. And Matthew was the one who had started the doubts in her mind. Matthew Craven, with clever words, repetitive words, putting pictures in her head, making her see things she had never wanted to see before——

The door opened, and it was almost seven-thirty, and he came in, frozen-looking, took his coat off and sat down. Siana stared at him as though he were a frightening stranger. He looked up and saw, and asked.

'What's the matter?'

She shook her head.

'Tell me. You looked at me as though I'd two heads.'

'My aunt phoned,' she said.

'I don't see the connection.'

'I'll get your meal. It's ready.'

'Never mind that,' he answered. 'What the hell's up now?'

'I can't begin to tell you.'

'You'd better try,' he said grimly.

'It's—difficult to put into words,' she sighed. 'It's you—you've made me doubt them—you put things in my head—oh, you're clever with your words, aren't you?'

Matthew was sitting very still, intent, listening. 'Go on,' he said, and he didn't sound angry, he sounded quite gentle, in fact. It gave Siana more confidence.

'It made me think, as I talked to her, or rather after, how she seemed almost relieved that I wouldn't be able to go to the village while they were away.' She sat down slowly at the table and looked at him. 'And afterwards, I started to think, and remember—other things.'

Matthew did something rather strange, but not unexpected. He reached over and took Siana's hand, very gently. The touch was warm and comforting.

'Then you must tell me what they are, when you want to,' he said. 'I'm glad I make you think.'

She half smiled. 'Why?'

'Because then I can help you.'

His words had an odd effect on her, a repeat of

something similar that he had said on his first visit that had made her nervous and dismayed. But now, somehow, they seemed right, and not at all frightening. 'I don't see how,' she said.

'You will, in time. And we have time.'

'You didn't order the snow, did you?' she asked, only half joking.

He smiled. 'I can't take the credit for that—no, but the timing was perfect.'

A suspicion had been growing, and now she voiced it. 'That day—yesterday, when you spoke to me on the beach and walked back with me—had you planned it?'

'Yes. And if I hadn't seen you I'd have found some other way of getting to talk to you. A neighbourly enquiry once the snow started—something—anything.' His eyes weren't smiling, they were serious. Siana's heart started beating very fast. She couldn't erase the fear, not just in a few moments, because he was being pleasant, and he was.

'Why me?' she asked. 'Why?'

'You'll see.'

She shook her head. 'You won't tell me anything——'

'Perhaps you're not ready to hear it yet. Is it so surprising to you that someone should want to talk to you? Have they given you that impression?'

'My aunt and uncle? I don't understand what you mean.'

'What have they said to you? About the villagers, for example.'

She shrugged. 'Nothing particularly. Except——'
she hesitated.

'Yes?'

'That—with it being an isolated community, as
it is, they're rather clannish—you know, strangers
not wanted, something like that. I've always
accepted it.'

'I didn't find it so when I came.'

'You're different,' she said bitterly.

'Pushing, you mean?' He half smiled, then stood
up. 'I'll dish out that food—I'm hungry! We can
talk while we eat. In what way am I different?
Apart from the rather obvious fact that I'm a man.'

'You're so—confident. You'd talk to anyone and
expect them to like you——' her voice tailed away.

'And you don't? Is that it? Why?'

'I don't know.' Siana shook her head. 'I'll help
you. I put two plates to warm in the grill.' It was
easier to be doing something instead of just sitting,
so she took the filled plates from him and put them
on the table.

'Hmm, looks good. Smells good. What is it? Beef
and dumplings?'

'Yes. Apple pie and cream to follow. On the top
there.'

They sat down to eat, and for a few minutes there
was silence, broken only by the crackling of the fire
and the faint hiss of the lamp. Siana was scarcely
aware of what she was eating. Her head was full of
chaotic thoughts and half surfacing memories of
things said and implied in the past two years. Some

were difficult to remember. She wished her memory of recent events were better. If only, she thought, I could think more clearly....

'Penny for them.'

She looked up from her apple pie. 'You wouldn't be interested.'

'Try me.'

'I was just going over what you'd said, about the villagers I mean, and how differently I saw everything from you. I was trying to sort out why.'

'And have you?'

'Not yet.'

'But you're rarely seen in the village, so how can you get to know anyone?'

'Don't confuse me further, please! Anyway, you know why.'

'I don't.'

'Well, you know—my leg—and my lost memory——'

'Yes. So?'

'I'm different from others——'

'My God!' She saw the sudden, startling anger in his face, and flinched.

'My God! Is that what they do to you? Tell you you're "different"?' The force of his words took her by surprise. She looked at him, shattered, not understanding the sudden flare of temper.

'But I am——'

He banged his fist on the table, making the plates rattle. 'No, dammit, you're not!'

'You wouldn't understand!' she flared. 'You don't know what it's like to feel only half a person because there's a huge blank where memories should be. Life's so straightforward to someone like *you*——'

'Then why do you resist help so strongly?' he flashed back.

'I don't! No one can do anything——'

'I suppose they told you that too!'

'What if they did? They're right, aren't they? I've tried to remember, I've tried desperately— there's nothing——'

'And there never will be if you let them smother you like they're doing now, not letting you talk to anyone only them, making sure nothing ever happens to jog you out of your mental lethargy——'

'I'm not going to stay here and listen to you!' she shouted. 'You're doing this deliberately to frighten me——'

'No, I'm not. But I'm making you come to life at last.' He stood up abruptly, came round to her, and hauled her to her feet. 'And by God, if it means using force, I will!' His eyes blazed at her.

'You're hurting me,' she whispered, shaken, trembling. 'Let me go—please!'

Instead he tightened his grip and pulled her towards him. For a moment her face was against the rough dark sweater he wore, and she could feel his heartbeat, strong and steady. Then he bent his head, put his arms tightly round her, and kissed her.

CHAPTER FOUR

His mouth came down on hers, and he wasn't being gentle—at first. He was hard and frightening and exciting all at once, all mixed up in the strange suddenness of an entirely new experience. Or was it? Something stirred in her mind, then was gone as she found herself responding to the growing depths of what had begun as a mere kiss. It was no longer that; it was fire and sensation and a surging in the blood, a tingling—a longing. And it was timeless.

He moved slightly away, releasing her from the sweet torture, and looked down at her and said huskily: 'We both needed that.'

'No,' she whispered. 'You had no right——'

'Your heart is pounding. Tell me it left you totally unmoved and then talk about me having no right. Have you never been kissed before?'

'How would I know?' She said, still trembling. 'Go away. Leave me!'

He smiled. 'We're here together, remember? Just the two of us—alone. So where do you expect me to go?'

'You—you promised——'

'That I wouldn't harm you. I won't. There's no harm in a kiss. It's the most natural thing in the world——'

'Not with perfect strangers!'

'Perfect? I'm not perfect. Neither are you——'

'You're a stranger. And don't split hairs. You know I didn't mean perfect in that sense——'

'How can we be strangers? We've talked, eaten together, we're sharing a situation that's not normal—no, Siana, we're not strangers. Not now.' He looked down at her and she wanted to cry out at what she saw in his eyes, but it was too late for that. She should never have let him stay, and now it was too late. They were alone together in a large house, cut off effectively from the outside world by a blanket of deadly yet beautiful snow, and they were going to spend the night under the same roof, and then the following day, and the day after that ... and no escape.

She ran her tongue over suddenly dry lips, and a strange sensation filled her body suffusing every part of her; it was a feeling she had never known before, since living here, and it was not entirely unpleasant. It was treacherous, dangerous, deadly dangerous—because she knew she wanted him to take her in his arms again. Her heart pounded at the realisation and she turned away, lest he should see, but he caught her arm and said, very gently:

'Perhaps you'd better show me my room.' It was as though, shockingly, he had read her thoughts, was aware of her inner turmoil, was using words, soft, innocent-seeming words—my room—nothing wrong with that, except it was where he would be sleeping, or perhaps lying awake, listening, waiting, waiting....

'I—not yet. I—er—want to make firelighters first,

and then there's the washing up—and did you bring
your radio?' If she was babbling it was because she
couldn't help it, because it was easier—and safer—
to think of very practical things like radios and
dishes.

'Yes. I also brought something else that may in-
terest you.' Matthew smiled before turning away to
fetch the bulging duffel bag from near the door,
and Siana thought, with dismay, I'm beginning to
read double meanings into everything he says. She
cleared the table of dishes and he put the bag on
it and began to unpack a veritable cornucopia—
a radio, a torch, half a dozen paperback books and
finally a large washleather bag and a roll of what
looked like thick parchment.

'My paints and some canvases,' he told her, tip-
ping the contents of the bag on to the table. 'You
don't mind if I do some painting while I'm here,
do you?' He began to unroll the canvases, and she
saw that there was an unfinished painting on one,
but it was in shadow. The shock came a second or
so later. Matthew waited his moment, until she
had picked up the tubes of poster paint, studied
the brushes, and put them down again.

'No wonder you were gone so long,' she remarked.
'Was the painting on an easel?'

'Yes. But dry, fortunately. Do you want to see
it?'

She didn't guess. How could she imagine what
she was going to see? There was no way to prepare
her for it. She watched as he unrolled the inner
canvas completely, and something stirred momen-

tarily—then he held it up, behind the light so that it was fully revealed—and she caught her breath and clutched the chair as if the room had suddenly tipped out of balance as she found herself looking at the face of a young woman, the face she looked at in the mirror every morning. Siana herself, smiling slightly back at her. She closed her eyes, then opened them because for a moment she knew it was her imagination—it couldn't be her. But it was.

'How——' she croaked. 'How did you——'

'I watched you, from a distance—and I watched you through binoculars. You never knew, did you?'

She sat down, abruptly, before her legs let her down. 'It really is—the likeness is just—I can't believe it!' Matthew laid the canvas down and it curled up, and her face vanished.

'I thought it would surprise you. I wanted to see your face when I showed it you. And now I don't need binoculars, do I?'

'May I?' She reached over and picked it up. It was unfinished, of course. The hair was only sketched in, as was the neck and shoulders. Her lips were only faint, pencilled in, but her eyes looked back at her, almost with a secret smile of recognition, and the eyebrows, featherlight, gently curved, could have been her own. She touched them carefully. 'But—how—from a distance——' she looked up, bewildered.

'I guessed. And now I see I guessed right. You have the face of a madonna, Siana. Not the temperament, but certainly the face.'

'No,' she shook her head, tried to smile. 'It's a very ordinary face——'

'To you perhaps, not to those who see you. Don't you *know* you're good-looking? Has no one ever told you how stunning you look?'

'I wouldn't remember, would I?' She looked up at him again. 'You do yourself an injustice. You're a fine artist.'

'Thank you.' He inclined his head modestly. 'Tomorrow, if you'll sit for me, I'll continue.'

She stood up and began to stack the dishes. 'Yes, I'll sit for you.' It was better this way: conversation nearly normal despite the totally stunning surprise of what had just happened. She couldn't imagine any more shocks. But then, she couldn't see into the future.

At ten o'clock she was feeling very tired, but at the same time reluctant to go to bed. The evening had passed surprisingly quickly. Matthew had asked questions, very sensible and logical questions about the hot water system—could the water be heated from the kitchen fire now that the immersion heater was no longer working and if not was there a fireplace with a back boiler so that they would always have hot water? Siana, to her shame, didn't know, and they had spent some time checking every downstairs fireplace—including the one in the large hall, to find, at last, that it was the one he had expected it to be, the kitchen fire that had a boiler at the back, and a handle part way up the chimney to draw the draught.

'Then we must keep a fire going day and night,' he said. 'It'll save a lot of trouble unless I can get the dynamo working. I'll stoke up before we go to bed and get up at five to replenish.'

'And if we leave a fire going in the hall as well it will keep the rest of the house from getting too cold.'

'Yes. Better get making firelighters. Er—if you want a bath while there's still plenty of really hot water in the tank, I suggest you have one tonight. It might be your last for a few days.'

It was eminently sensible, of course, and Siana went up at nine-thirty and enjoyed a good soak, then found her oldest, most sensible dressing gown, a blue one that buttoned from neck to toes, made of thick wool and as shapeless as a sack. He had taken a brief look at it, grinned, and turned away when she returned to the kitchen at almost ten.

'I'm making us a cup of tea,' he said. 'Okay?'

'Okay. Thanks.' She went over to the sink and found her bottle of iron pills, and shook one out.

'What are those?' he asked, mildly curious.

'Iron pills. I'm anaemic.'

'May I see?'

She shrugged, 'They all look the same,' but handed him the bottle.

He opened it and took one out, then looked at her. 'Iron?' he queried. 'Are you sure? There's no label.'

'It's an old bottle,' she answered. 'Of course I'm sure! What on earth are you getting at?'

He didn't answer but filled the teapot with the boiling water, went over to the table and examined the pill by the lamplight. Siana followed, more amused than annoyed, and watched as he bit on the yellow pill and tasted it. 'What *are* you doing?' she asked at last.

'Just seeing if it is iron.

'Well?'

'It's not.'

'Don't be stupid! I should know, I take them every day——'

'How many?'

'Three. Morning, lunchtime, bedtime.'

'And does the doctor prescribe them for you?'

'Well, no——Uncle Peter's friend's a chemist in Glasgow——it saves having to keep getting a prescription, they're only cheap——look, what *is* this? The Spanish Inquisition or something?' She was beginning to feel annoyed and perturbed.

'This is a tranquilliser, Siana. There's no iron in it at all——all it does to you is keep you slightly doped all the time——'

'Don't be ridiculous!' she snapped. 'I've never heard of anything so——'

'Believe me.' He stared hard at her, angry, eyes dark. 'Believe me, I'm speaking the truth. I know exactly what these are. They're a medium strength tranquilliser, the normal dose of which is one or two a day, and you're taking *three*.'

'But——but I——' she was stammering with shock and confusion. 'How can they be?'

'Quite easily,' he said grimly, 'If your uncle has an obliging chemist friend who thinks they're for him, or your aunt—probably both, with the amount you're getting through.'

She was silenced by the vehemence of his words, the force—and the hard anger. Slowly she sat down. 'Why?' she asked. 'Why would they do that to me?'

'I'm sorry, Siana,' he said gently. 'Here, drink your tea, but don't take that. It's all part of the pattern, don't you see? The desire to keep you here with them, quiet and peaceful—and away from others.'

'But why?' she persisted. She began to feel almost ill at the thought, the implications of his words.

'God knows. But look at it with me for a moment. You're easily confused, you don't remember anything of your past life—you know little of your present one, save that you're well looked after. If you're taking those—and you are—that's precisely the effect they'll have. You're used to them as well, so the process is continual. This bottle's nearly full. Tell me, what did they say before they went— about these, I mean?'

Siana tried to remember, frowning. 'My aunt said not to forget to take them three times a day, they were essential for my health—I didn't take one at lunch! I forgot with all the things happening.'

'And this afternoon you got really angry with me—you sparked into life, remember?' She nodded slowly. 'The effect of the morning one had worn off. Give me that one, please.'

She handed it to him and Matthew tipped the pills into his hand and held them for a moment. 'I'm going to burn them,' he said.

'No, you can't—what if you're mistaken——' she gasped.

'I'm not, and you know it. If you still doubt me, give me the name of your uncle's friend.'

'What will you do?'

'Telephone him.'

'But what will you say?'

He smiled slightly. 'Enough. Enough to make him tell me the truth. You can listen if you want.'

But she already knew that it wouldn't be necessary. She shook her head. 'You don't need to,' she whispered. 'I believe you.'

She watched him fling them on the fire where they sparked briefly before vanishing into the hot coals. It was as though she had just taken a large step. And something deep within her told her that it was the first of many.

She sighed. 'I suppose I'll lay awake for hours now——' She stopped, realising what she had said.

'You may for one night, but you'll soon adjust,' he said. 'Take the torch and read if you want. I brought you some books. I hope you've got a few for me.'

'Plenty.' She picked up the selection he had brought. They were well read, not new, and not at all what she had expected. But then she didn't know what she had expected. She didn't know his taste. There were two detective novels, a book of modern poetry, a few books of short stories by well known writers, and the last—that was the one that made her pause, her mouth tightening helplessly, then look up at him, holding it.

'Is this some kind of joke?' she asked. 'Because I don't find it very funny.'

'No.' He took the book from her, its title, one word, stark black against a grey background. *Amnesia.* 'It's not a joke—it's certainly not meant to be funny. It's for you to read.'

'And I suppose it provides the instant key for restoring memory? Read two chapters and bingo! all is revealed.'

'It's a serious book, written by an expert psychiatrist to explain the many reasons for loss of memory. It could help.'

Matthew put it back with the others on the table. 'No one's going to force you to read it, but there it is if you want to.'

'Thanks.' She deliberately picked a book of short stories. 'I think I'll go to bed now. Is there anything you want to ask before I go?'

He looked around the room. 'No. Mind if I stay up a while?'

'Stay as late as you like.'

'I'll keep a fire in.'

'Goodnight.'

'Goodnight, Siana.' She walked out and left him. She had previously found two hot water bottles, offered one to Matthew, who had refused it with a smile and the answer that he never felt the cold in bed or anywhere else. Siana had filled them both for herself, and now she slid into a deliciously warm bed and, checking that the candle was safe in its holder, began to read. It was an ornate red candle, strictly for ornamental purposes, and usually in a silver candelabrum in the dining room, but Aunt Peggy would surely understand. The light was only dim, and Siana found the effort of straining to see the words too much for her. After a few pages she blew out the candle and lay down to watch the whirling snow fall in a constant and never-ending pattern outside. The air in her bedroom was cold, getting colder, but her body was warm, the bed was very comfortable, and she found it an effort to keep her eyes open. The snow had an hypnotic effect, so gentle, persistent, ever changing, yet somehow ever the same....

She awoke, much surprised to find that she had actually been asleep. All was still and quiet in the house. It was too much effort to look—or try to look—at her bedside alarm, and she lay there for a few moments wondering what had woken her. There had been something, something elusive, on the other side of sleep, far away, a fragment of a dream——

No sound, nothing. Yet there had been—something. Then she heard it again, and knew what had woken her. A groan of pain followed by a brief, wordless exclamation as something clattered to the floor. The noise could only come from Matthew's room opposite hers. Siana froze in brief fear—then, finding her voice, called: Matthew? Is that you?'

The only answer was a further groan, then, faintly: 'Siana?' It was a cry for help. She fumbled for her dressing gown, put it on and ran out of her room. His door was wide open. She hesitated at the door.

'Matthew?' It was difficult to distinguish anything save a vague dark blur where his bed was.

'I'm—in bed. I'm sorry, did I wake you?'

'What is it?' She walked over and found the matches on his bedside chair and lit his candle. He lay on his back, face contorted with pain, then managed a weak grin.

'My damned back—look, I'll be all right——' he winced, teeth clenched, and put out a hand to hers. 'Don't—don't stay—get back to bed—you'll freeze——'

'But I can't leave you,' she said, anguished. 'What's the matter with your back?'

'I can't move—it's—I should have had that bottle you offered. It's nothing, just an injury I once had playing rugger—it sometimes locks——' he stopped and gripped her hand tightly.

'Wait, let me go. I'll get you my bottles.' His hand was icy cold. She eased herself gently free and hurried out to her bedroom to return with the still hot bottles. 'I'll put one either side, then I'll go and make you a hot drink.' She slid one either side of him, careful not to touch him, and he smiled at her.

'Thanks.'

'I'll not be a minute. Stay there and don't try to move.'

He grimaced. 'I couldn't if I wanted to.'

Siana took his candle to light her way down, filling the kettle and waited impatiently for it to boil. He'd thought it cissyish to have a bottle, and this was probably the result. She wondered what the injury had been. A slipped disc? His hand had been so cold, almost icy. She suddenly realised how helpless she would be if he were to become ill. What was it people suffered from when there was no heat and their body temperature dropped? She searched her mind for the word—hypothermia, that was it. And it could be dangerous, and he'd assured her he never felt the cold which perhaps made it worse. She began to shiver, cold herself, and went to stoke up the fire with more coal. That was even more essential now.

She made two cups of scalding hot coffee and carried them carefully up, taking a torch instead of the candle, because it was safer for him.

'Shall I try and sit you up?' she asked.

'No, I couldn't.' His teeth began to chatter, and he shivered. 'I'm so cold.'

'Oh, please—please—let me get you an extra blanket——'

'No, don't leave me.' He clutched her arm. 'It wouldn't help—so cold——' his voice tailed away. 'My back—oh God, my back!'

'Can I do anything?'

'Nothing—only expert massage sometimes clears it. I used to go to a physiotherapist—not had this for so long—thought it had gone——'

'Here, try and sip some coffee.' She leaned over and lifted his head very slowly and carefully. 'Say if it hurts.'

'That's—ouch! fine——' he sipped gratefully and then sank back on to his pillow. 'Thanks.'

Siana was frightened. He was so helpless, and she had never expected to see him helpless. It threw her out of balance as she realised how much she had come to rely on him in such a short time. 'Look,' she said tentatively, 'if I can help in any way—rub your back, even, just say. I'll do anything to help.'

'You're kind.' He managed a faint smile. 'But I don't know—it may do more harm than good. If only I weren't so cold—so cold——'

'I'm going to get you the eiderdown off my bed,' she said, and left him before he could refuse. She brought it back and laid it over his covers.

'Have I got a temperature?' he asked. His voice was definitely weaker. Siana put her hand on his forehead and was shocked at how icy and damp it was. Please God, don't let him die, she prayed silently.

'It's—normal, I think,' she lied desperately. 'Try and drink more coffee.' She was beginning to feel the cold herself, her fingers growing more numb by the minute. There had been a recent case in the papers of two climbers lost on a mountain in freezing conditions who had been rescued in the nick of time; they had spent seven hours huddled in a single sleeping bag, and that had saved their lives. Their own shared body heat had saved them. But she wasn't on an icy mountain, and this was a strange man—who had kissed her. She hadn't forgotten that; she never would. Yet he was helpless, and immobile.

'Are the bottles helping?' she asked him. He didn't answer for a moment.

'Bottles?'

'I put two bottles in. Shall I fill them again?' she should have done that straight away of course.

'What bottles? Whisky?'

She looked at him in faint horror. If he was delirious—— 'I'll—I'll take them and fill them. Do you want a drop of whisky?'

He looked blankly at her, then closed his eyes. 'Whisky?' he repeated.

She took the hot water bottles out and went downstairs in the dark, lit the candle and the gas, and refilled the kettle. Now she was really worried. Before, when she had been down to make his coffee, she had merely been concerned at his condition, but she had seen the rapid change in him—and only she could help him. There was no one else, no aunt or uncle to tell her exactly what to do, to take control and reassure her—only Siana herself, and she was afraid of what might happen. She knew now what she must do. If Matthew were no better when she returned to the bedroom with the bottles, she knew what she had to do. She had no choice.

She filled them and felt her way up in the dark, and her resolve strengthened with each step. He lay there, very still, eyes closed, and she went over to his bed and looked at him. Then she bent over him and put her hand on his face. It was very cold.

'It's all right,' she whispered. 'Don't worry, I'll take care of you.' Very gently she slid in bed beside him, put one bottle at his feet, the other at his other side, and snuggled up to him. 'I'll keep you warm. Do you hear me, Matthew?'

'Mmm. Cold—so cold.'

'You won't be soon. I've filled the bottles—and I'll stay with you.'

She had kept on her dressing gown, and that was additional warmth for them both. The bed was four foot wide, not quite a double, but wide enough for comfort, and she began to feel warmth suffusing her after a minute or so, and her relief was overwhelming. It was working; that was something. She too lay very still alongside Matthew, arms up in front of her instinctively, and touching his arm. He hadn't noticed or spoken; he might not even realise she was there. They were both getting warmer as the minutes passed, and she reached up tentatively and touched his face. His skin was more a normal temperature, and no longer damp, and he had stopped shivering. She knew then that she had done the right thing, the only thing, to help him. Then gradually, as sleep overcame her, the thought came to her, diffused and from far away, that she had never been so comfortable—or safe— as she was at that moment. That was the last coherent thought before she slept.

When she woke the room was nearly light. Matthew's arm lay across her, and they had been sleeping facing each other, noses almost touching, so close that she could feel his breath on her face. He was breathing steadily and deeply, and he was very warm. She knew she must get up, but oddly,

she didn't really want to move. It was so absolutely
wonderful—and that was a very horrifying thought
to have. She had no right to be lying there feeling
so comfortable with this dark stranger she scarcely
knew. What was it he had said? 'How can we be
strangers? We've talked, eaten together——' and
now he could have added, 'and shared a bed.' She
went cold inside at the thought, and must have
moved slightly, for he opened his eyes and looked
at her.

'Hello,' he said. 'This is nice——' He looked
very puzzled but not at all dismayed. Siana
wondered if she had gone as fiery red as she felt.

'How are you?' she asked. For some reason she
couldn't move, and realised why a moment later
as she realised the weight on her legs was one of
his legs. This needed a bit of untangling. She wondered why she felt so reluctant to move.

'My back's killing me——' Matthew bit his lip.
'I can't—damn well move——'

'Oh!' So how did she get out of that?

'Did you—was I—er—ill or something? I
mean——' he grinned as if embarrassed.

'You were very cold, and delirious——'

'Was I? Good grief! I'm never ill.'

'You were, I promise you. Look—er—Matthew,
I'd better——'

He gave a shout of pain, cutting off her words.
Then: 'Oh—sorry, Siana, did I scare you? Oh God,
this back of mine! Look, I hate to ask—you've done
so much—but could you sort of ease yourself over

and get your hand on my back and rub it?' His face contorted, he bit his lip.

'I—won't it do more harm? I don't know anything about massage. Wouldn't I be better getting out? I mean——'

'No. I can't move my damned leg! I'm sorry to ask——'

'It's all right.' She freed her arm, put it round him, and eased up his pyjama jacket. The whole situation was bizarre in the extreme. She wished she were anywhere but there—no, she didn't——

'There?' she asked.

'No. Higher, up a bit, left. Ah—ouch!—there. Can you rub gently?'

She began to do so, and heard his sigh. 'Ah—yes, that's it. Yes—a bit firmer—I think I can stand it——'

His back was hard and straight—and very tense. She could feel the muscles tauten under her hand. 'Relax,' she said. 'Try and relax——'

'I'm trying, but it's locked. Can you move over more?'

'No, your leg's too heavy. If you moved your leg——' she began.

'I can't,' he cut in. 'But you're doing a power of good. I can feel—your hand's so warm and comforting. You're a natural masseuse, Siana. Ah, that's it—ah!' He sighed. 'Just there.'

Her hand was aching, her arm was aching. It was hard work. And they were too close for comfort. She certainly couldn't relax. She was tense in every muscle, resisting a terrible impulse that was coming over her, fighting something she didn't understand, and frightened he would feel, as well as hear, the erratic thudding of her heart.

Then, as inevitable as breathing, and at the moment she knew he would, he kissed her. It was a very gentle kiss.

CHAPTER FIVE

'THANK you,' Matthew whispered. For one moment she had instinctively responded, then, dismayed, she pulled her face away from his.

'Oh,' she said, 'I——'

He kissed her again, and she could feel his back, under her hand, warm and strong, and his arm, which had been round her, tightened imperceptibly, and this time the kiss was not so gentle, but it was more delightful and she didn't break away because she couldn't anyway—and she didn't now want to. She didn't care any more about the fact that she should be getting out of his bed fast, it no longer seemed important, it no longer seemed to matter—and when he forced her mouth open her only response at first was a murmur and then a soundless, wordless answering with her own mouth as the kiss deepened and became more than a kiss. It became a warmth and a fire that took over and overwhelmed her, and now she knew, deep down inside her, that there was to be no moving away, only a moving closer still. Matthew knew it too, and his leg, the one he hadn't been able to move, was pressing against her very hard, imprisoning her, and his muscular strength was clearly recovered and she managed to wonder, vaguely, as he began to unbutton her dressing gown, if his miracle recovery was due to her rubbing his back. Then it seemed a question of total irrelevance in the light of what was now happening to her, which was totally delightful and like nothing that had ever happened to her before.

Some distant memory stirred, and was gone as he slid his arms around her and began caressing her with an expertise that left her totally without any resistance. She moaned softly, and his lips silenced her, then he whispered: 'Close your eyes, my darling,' and she did so, her heart thudding uncontrollably, and waiting, waiting—wanting she knew not what, and too late to care now, yet knowing exactly, knowing too that the point of no return had been reached, and passed. His lips were warm on her neck, on her breast, and she turned and lay on her back and pulled him to her and gave herself to the ecstasy of his hands and mouth and body.

They were on fire, and nothing in the world could put the fire out now. Crying, sobbing incoherently, a mixture of bliss and sweet, sweet pain, and movement and deep, primitive surging and longing—and still a waiting, a building up to an inevitable end that could not, must not be postponed or she would die. She scratched his back and cried out something, she knew not what, and for a brief moment saw his face, poised above her, the face of a man reaching his limits of patience, and she closed her eyes in agony, sweet precious agony, then the world was blotted out, and all was sensation, and feeling and movement, and she was lost.

An eternity later she lay there basking in an afterglow, suffused, sated, and Matthew lay beside her, and there were no words needed, and none spoken. Then, so gradually she was scarcely aware of it, shame filled her, and she moved away from him and tried to sit up, pulling a sheet up with her, and kept her eyes averted from him and began to get out of bed. He caught her.

'No!' she exclaimed fiercely. 'Let me go—oh, let me *go*—I can't—oh God!'

'Don't fight,' he said. 'See, it's all right, see——' He pulled the sheet from her and pulled her down to him again. She saw his eyes, dark with renewed desire, and she felt sick and frightened, and struggled to free herself, but in vain.

'I want you,' he muttered, and her struggles only served to excite him, she could see that. 'I want you again—and now——'

'No—let me go——' She was weakening, the treacherous weakness of her own body betraying her, her own arms ceasing to resist his absolute control of her, and her body, the betrayer, responding to the movement of his as she was pulled down, and down, sinking into the warmth beside him, fighting feebly now, a token protest only as the longing for him overcame the shame. He began to kiss her and tease her with his fingers, and the fire which had subsided started burning again, this time more fiercely than before. He made love to her again, and it was gentler and her response greater, and nothing else in the whole world mattered any more.

Siana stood in the kitchen. She had left Matthew

sleeping in the bed they had shared in the fullest sense of the word. The shame that had filled her before, after that first time, was as nothing compared to her feelings now. She hated herself and she hated him for what he had done to her, and if she was to retain her sanity it must never be allowed to happen again. What did he think of her now? As a lonely, frustrated woman who would leap into bed with the first man who asked her? He hadn't even asked her. Her face felt white and drawn and she put her hand to her cheek to feel its smooth coldness. She had got into bed with him—to warm him, to help save him from illness, as she had thought. But he, not remembering, must not have seen it that way.

I was mad, she thought, utterly crazy to do a thing like that. But at the same time she knew it was no use. Too late for regrets. It had happened. Matthew had made love to her, not once but twice, and she had responded fully both times, she couldn't even deny it to herself. He had woken her senses, aroused her to the pitch of awareness and desire beyond which nothing else counted, and had taken her with expertise to a region of sheer sensuality. He was an animal, a strong lustful animal, and with her he had slaked his lust. She struck the edge of the table with her hand, and the pain was sharp enough to make her cry out, but it wasn't sharp enough to dim the memories of her own desire for him and her own unbridled response that had sent him surging to an explosive climax. She rubbed her hand and a sob rose in her throat. She wanted to run out, to run away never to return—but she was trapped within the four walls of the house with him for now and for as long as the snow lasted.

She went to open the back door, to feel the air on her face, and the snow was half way up the door, a thick white, impenetrable wedge. The air was icy cold, stinging her cheeks and hands, but it was fresh and clean—and she felt dirty. She felt as if she would never be clean again. Matthew had used her to satisfy his animal needs, and never again would she be safe from him; she had no illusions about that. He would take her when he wanted her. It was cold, standing at the door, and she buttoned up her dressing gown, her mind rejecting the sharp memory of him unbuttoning it, one button at a time, slowly, mockingly, teasing her, arousing himself at the same time—'Stop it!' she cried, and put her hand to her mouth as if to stifle the imaginings. His hands were strong and large and powerful enough to crush the life out of her if he chose, but he had put them to different use and he knew what he was doing, he had known precisely what he was doing from the first time he had kissed her. She wondered how many women he had made love to——

'Siana! You'll freeze.' His voice cut in on her thoughts and she whirled round, nearly falling, clutching at the door. He had been asleep. She had been careful not to wake him because she needed to be alone. Matthew walked slowly across the kitchen towards her, and she looked at him and it was like seeing a stranger, a complete stranger, a beast. Wide-eyed, unable to move away, she watched him close the door. He had dressed, he needed a shave, his hair was tousled, and he looked tired. Siana began to tremble. She knew why he looked tired, she knew everything about him, and she wished she didn't. She wished she were dead.

He touched her arm, and she flinched as if he had branded her. 'I'm going to make a cup of coffee,' he said. 'I could do with one.' He smiled at her, warmth in his eyes—that and knowledge of her. She turned away, feeling sick.

'What is it?' he asked, voice soft.

'You—how can you ask?' she whispered. 'Oh God, don't *touch* me again!' She was trembling, and she went to the table and sat down.

'Because we made love? Is that why?'

He had said the words. How could he? Made love, as though they were lovers, as though they loved each other.

'We didn't,' she said flatly. 'I should never have let you touch me. I should have got up while I was safe. I only got in to help you—you were ill—and that's how you—you thank me.' She was near to tears.

'Was I wrong then?' he said harshly. 'Did I imagine that response? Did I rape you—force myself on you? Oh no, Siana, I didn't. You knew what was happening all right and you enjoyed it, don't kid yourself you didn't. You discovered you're a woman, that's what happened, and now you're trying to deny it. Why? You *are* a woman. You were in bed with me, and I kissed you. Did you think I was made of stone or something? I'm not—and neither are you. What happened after that is older than time and as natural and inevitable as time itself——'

'Shut up! I don't want to hear——' she began.

Matthew pulled her to her feet, not roughly, and held her. 'Don't play the outraged virgin,' he snapped, 'because you're not. You're not now—and you weren't before——'

'How dare you!' Incensed, she wrenched her hand free and struck him hard across his face. 'How *dare* you!' It was a nightmare, endless, terrible.

'I dare to speak the truth,' the mark whitened on his cheek, then dulled, 'only you don't want to hear it. Your response was that of a woman, not a girl——'

'I won't listen!' She jerked away from him. 'Don't touch me again. Don't ever touch me!'

'I don't think you even mean that.' He smiled. 'We're alone here, remember? And by the look of that snow outside, it'll be for a week at least. And you'll lie in your bed at night, and you'll remember——'

'I won't!'

'You won't be able to help yourself. You'll want me as much as I want you.' His eyes—she couldn't look away from the eyes which held hers. Dark eyes that held all the knowledge of her. She didn't want to look at them, but she was helpless. 'And we'll make love again, don't think we won't. That's a promise.' He turned away and began to fill the kettle. Siana stood motionless by the table. His words had had the strangest effect on her, almost as if any decisions were taken out of her control. He told her quite plainly that he would make love to her—and she knew already that he was a man who always got what he wanted. He wanted her. It was quite simple really, because she had no choice. There was no escape, and he was infinitely stronger than her and when he wanted her he would have her. And she knew what the effect of his words was, in her innermost self; she knew, but her mind denied it.

She took a deep breath and sat down again. 'I'm going to make breakfast for you,' said Matthew. 'Why don't you go and get dressed? You'll feel warmer with some clothes on.' He spoke as normally as if nothing had happened, moving about, opening the cupboard to get the pan out, beginning to whistle softly. Siana looked at him helplessly. What was it about him that so confused her? It was the sheer normality of his behaviour, as *though nothing had happened*. Yet he'd just changed her whole life, that was all. And there was nothing she could do about that. Absolutely nothing.

She walked out, went up to her bedroom and began to dress. She looked at her bed, virtually unslept in, and pulled up the covers. On her way out she glanced in as if drawn by a magnet towards the room they had spent the night in. Matthew had made the bed, it was neat and tidy. She looked away hastily. No, she didn't want to think about it. She ran downstairs again, and into the kitchen.

The fire was burning brightly, the pan sizzled on the stove, and the kettle was boiling. Matthew said cheerfully: 'Sit down. I'll see if I can get the dynamo working today. Breakfast's nearly ready, I'll go after. You'd better stay in here. It's nearly nine, would you switch on the radio, please? We'll get the news.'

Wordlessly Siana obeyed and pop music floated out into the room. She went to get knives and forks. Matthew accompanied the music in a tuneful whistle and Siana sat at the table. He turned round and looked at her. 'Tea or coffee?'

It was like a dream now, not a nightmare. He really was acting as if everything were quite normal. And the sooner she fell in with the charade the better for her inner turmoil.

'Coffee, please. Shall I——'

'No, I can manage. Sit there and just listen. Let's see what the rest of Great Britain is doing.'

The news came on as he gave her her plate of fish, and she waited, fork poised, as the announcer read out what they already knew. The whole of the north of Britain was blanketed in snow, all roads closed, emergency helicopter services fully employed in looking after isolated farmhouses and communities. A state of emergency had been declared and work was going on to reopen trunk roads. There was a strike of railwaymen in Brighton—He switched off. 'We'll save the batteries,' he said. He looked at her. 'You heard. It's bad almost everywhere. We've got food and warmth, let's keep it that way. We don't know exactly how long we'll be stranded, so I'm going to check all foodstuffs and if we have to go on rations, we will. And if the waterpipes freeze we'll melt snow for drinks. Okay? Any comments?'

Siana shook her head. He had everything orga-
nised—including me, she thought bitterly.

'Right. Dynamo first, food after. While I'm outside I suggest you look round and see if you've any
more candles.'

She nodded. 'Lost your tongue?' Matthew enquired.

'No. You have everything under control. There's
not much for me to say, is there?'

He looked steadily at her. 'We won't starve, and
we won't die of cold, and we won't fall downstairs
and break our necks in the dark because we've no
light. Now if you think I'm being over-zealous, feel
free to say so.' His voice was hard, as hard as his
face. Not like it had been before——

'No,' she said hastily. 'I'm sorry. You're right, of
course.'

'I'm glad you think so. Eat up before your fish
gets cold. One more meal of this. I won't be sorry
when we finish it. I could even look foward to beans
on toast for a change.'

'There won't be any bread after today.'

'You've got flour, haven't you?'

'Yes, but there's no yeast.'

'Ever heard of soda bread? That's easy. If you
can't make it, I will.' He smiled at her. 'You'll want
for nothing.'

Siana got up quickly and took her plate to the
sink. His words were ambiguous, double-edged. She
sensed it was deliberate, but she knew better now
than to challenge him. A strange feeling, almost of
calm, had come over her. She had no choice but

to accept the inevitable situation they were in. She had heard the news, and almost everywhere else was as badly off—probably worse. Matthew was right! they had ample supplies, and warmth—and he made the decisions, and he was going to try and restore the electricity soon, and plan their eating, and all she had to do was go along with it. It was easier than fighting, she hadn't the strength for that. But she didn't want to think about night-time. Not yet. She needn't think about that for at least twelve hours. An idea had come to her, a mere glimmer as yet, but she wanted to think about it....

It was late afternoon, and all the work for the day had been done. The dynamo was totally out of action, even the water to it now having frozen over so that none ran. They had ample food for four weeks, for the two of them, by which time the snow would have either gone or snowploughs would have reached the village, and, Matthew told her cheerfully, he would have constructed a pair of skis by then and would get there somehow. They were going to have a slap-up three-course dinner—and then, tomorrow, a more spartan but nutritionally adequate diet would commence. It was all planned. Siana had found a dozen plain wax candles and a box of nightlights at the back of a cupboard. They had three boxes of matches left, would not use them except in emergency, lighting both stove and candles from paper spills, and as the fire was to be kept alight at all times it was unlikely that the matches would be needed. She had occupied herself mak-

ing several dozen tight paper spills while Matthew
turned all inessential taps off round the house, leaving them the ones in the kitchen and bathroom
only.

She had looked out an old chess set after he had
asked her if she played, and she wasn't sure if she
had ever learned; she certainly couldn't remember
that. But it might be an interesting experiment to
see if the moves came back to her once they had
started. She looked at the clock and decided to prepare the sumptuous, slap-up three-course dinner—
Scotch broth, followed by chicken and roast potatoes
with all the trimmings followed by strawberry
mousse, coffee and liqueurs. The chicken was a
large tinned one, and they would curry what was
left tomorrow, and she had already prepared the
mousse from beaten egg whites, sugar and tinned
strawberries, well crushed. She had put the two
dishes outside on the window ledge packed round
by snow, an ideal refrigerator now that there was
no electricity. Matthew was lighting the fire in
the hall, she could hear him whistling as though
he hadn't a care in the world. She wondered if there
was ever any situation with which he couldn't cope,
and doubted it. She knew nothing about him, save
that he could paint well, and had lived in Marine
Cottage for several months, and often went fishing
in the early morning. After that, nothing. Yet he
knew as much about her as she herself did.

The telephone shrilled and she turned the gas off
so as not to waste it, and went into the hall to
answer it. Matthew knelt by the fireplace coaxing

life into reluctant wood, and didn't look round as she picked up the telephone.

The line was appalling, with distant whirrs and voices so that most of her aunt's words were lost. It was a relief to Siana, since her discovery that she had been fed tranquillisers by the two people she trusted most she had been worried about keeping her tone natural during her aunt's nightly call. No deception was necessary. Both had to shout to be heard, and Siana assured her aunt that all was well, surely the biggest lie she had ever told, and then, mercifully, the call was over. She put the telephone back on the rest.

'I'm getting dinner ready,' she told Matthew.

'Good. Need any help?'

'No. I work better alone.' She left him and went back into the kitchen. Two candles on the window-sill provided the light for her to work by. The kitchen was warm and comfortable, the fire crackled merrily in the hearth, and the plates warmed beside it. This was her home, and had been for two years, and she had never been in it without her aunt and uncle before. She had always felt so safe with them, but had it been a fool's paradise? She wasn't safe with Matthew Craven, she was by no means safe, as had already been proved, and yet in one day she had become aware of having her world turned topsy-turvy by him, by all he had said and done, and somehow it seemed that in a most odd way they were the threat, and he was—what was he? He was a man who had entered her life and made her aware of herself, in so many ways. Perhaps in destroying those pills he had done more than he knew; she wasn't yet sure.

The potatoes were nearly ready, the gravy simmering. She opened the window to fetch in the mousse, and icy air blasted in, fluttering the candles madly before extinguishing them. 'Damn,' she muttered, relit them from the gas, carried them to the table, and called Matthew, who had vanished after finishing the hall fire.

His voice floated down from upstairs. 'Down in a moment.'

She dished everything up, and when it was ready he walked in. He had shaved and combed his hair. 'I was going to put on my dinner jacket, seeing that this is our last luxury meal,' he said, 'but my valet's mislaid it.'

He could joke as though everything was just so. Siana wondered what kind of man he really was—and decided to find out. The simplest way of all was to ask. She waited her moment, when he was enjoying his food.

'You never mentioned where you lived before you came to Marine Cottage,' she said. 'Was it far away?'

'I come originally from London,' he answered, 'but I've been travelling round for a while.' He smiled faintly. 'Why do you ask?'

'You know everything about me, yet you're a mystery. Put it down to sheer nosiness, if you like.'

'Perfectly natural.' He helped himself to more potatoes. 'This is delicious. A meal to remember—

and let's face it, that's what we'll have to do. After today it's emergency rations.'

She shuddered. 'You make it sound awfully grim.'

'No, we'll eat well, never fear. It may test our ingenuity. I mean, how many ways are there to cook oats?'

'We'll find out, won't we?' He had somehow changed the subject—she was more determined to return to it. 'Why were you "travelling around" as you put it? Was it to do with your work?'

'Partly.'

'As a painter?'

'That's more a hobby than anything. By profession I'm a photographer.'

'Oh!' That was a surprise. He didn't look like any photographer she'd ever seen. 'What kind? Weddings? Newspaper work?'

'No. Models, fashion photos for magazines. It was quite a lucrative line of work.'

'Then why did you stop?' she asked.

He looked across the table at her. The candlelight gentled and softened his features, and he was a different man with the shadows emphasising his strong bone structure. 'It no longer pleased me,' he said quietly.

It was a strange answer. She felt a small shiver touch the back of her neck at the words—and at the way he said them. There was more, much more than he was saying, and quite suddenly she didn't want to know. It was not time for her to know. Something had entered that room, and it surrounded them, and it was a shimmering growing of a kind of tension that was timeless and inexplicable, as though she were on the brink of something that might alter her life yet again. There had been too many disturbances, she wasn't ready for any more.

She stood up. 'I'll get the mousse—I put it outside on the ledge. We don't need a fridge, it's freezing out there.' It was essential not to think, not to hear again those words that echoed silently in her brain. 'It no longer pleased me.'

'It looks delicious.' She waited until he had finished his chicken and they both took the first spoonful of mousse together.

'Oh! Ouch——' they looked at each other, then started laughing. It was colder than ice cream—frozen solid. 'Oh, I'm sorry,' she said, when she could speak.

'No matter. Five minutes in the hearth should effect a cure. Let me make the coffee while they thaw out. Did you get the liqueurs?'

'Yes. Cointreau or Drambuie?'

'I have a choice? The service in this restaurant is quite superb. Drambuie, I think. And you?'

'The same.'

Half an hour later all was cleared away, and the rest of the evening stretched ahead, and it must be filled, because she couldn't bear the waiting. It was better to occupy her mind. 'Can we play chess?' she asked. 'I'd like to know if I ever played before.'

'You can't remember?'

'No, not yet. But I might.'

'We'll see. Shall I light the paraffin lamp?'

'No, the candles will suffice if we sit at the table.'

'As you wish.' Matthew set out the board, and Siana watched. So far nothing registered. He looked at her. 'Ready?' he enquired.

She shook her head. 'Well, I know they're set out, I know that's a king,' she touched as she spoke. 'That's a queen—a knight—those are pawns—but nothing's registering yet.'

'It will. See, we'll have a trial run, I'll explain what moves you can make with each piece, and see if anything comes to you.' He began to explain, moving, showing her by example, and Siana felt some memory stirring as he spoke, as she watched his hands, careful, gentle hands—then suddenly, almost like something clicking inside her head, she knew. It all made sense. She remembered.

'Yes, oh yes!' she exclaimed. 'Of course!' It was like a light shining into a darkened room. She knew. 'Wait, it's coming back to me now.'

He nodded. 'I knew it would. Right, your move. Take it slowly at first. You've had a shock—take time to adjust. You realise, Siana, what's happened, don't you?'

'I've remembered something from beyond the last two years.'

'And there'll be more. Hold that thought in your mind. There'll be more, much more.' His eyes were steadily upon her. She felt as if she were drowning in them, in the depths she saw, but she was no longer afraid.

'Yes,' she answered. She lifted up her hand,

touched a pawn, and moved it two squares ahead. 'Let's go,' she said.

The game had tired her. The fact that she had lost was immaterial. The surge of awareness, of memory, was overwhelming and almost frightening. She sat white-faced by the fire and Matthew made her a hot cup of coffee and poured a full liqueur glass of Drambuie. 'Drink that, then your coffee,' he told her. 'Then have another liqueur.'

She sat back in the easy chair. 'It was like a door opening in my head,' she said. 'There's no other way to explain it.'

'I know,' he said. 'Don't rush it.'

'How would you know?' she asked, too tired to smile.

'You saw the book I brought? The one you thought in bad taste, titled *Amnesia*?'

'Yes. What about it?'

'I've read it. It says this kind of thing can happen. Something can trigger off a memory—it's happened to you. Let it happen, don't resist.'

'But why?' she asked, bewildered.

'Why what?'

'Why you—why should you want to help me?'

'Because you're a fellow human being, that's why,' he said lightly. But Siana knew there was something more. Much, much more. She didn't know what it was.

CHAPTER SIX

IT was bedtime. She could no longer stay awake. She knew that she would fall asleep in the chair if she didn't move. The chess over and the board put away, everything was tidy for morning—and it had begun to snow again. Matthew, reading a book by the light of a candle at the other side of the fire, said: 'Why don't you go to bed? You're nearly asleep.'

You know why, she wanted to cry, but she kept the words back. 'I'm shattered after that game,' she said instead. 'I'll—go.' She stood and went to the sink. 'Do you want a bottle?'

'Perhaps I better had. Can you manage with one?'

I'd sleep on a bed of nails in the snow if it meant you'd leave me alone, she thought. 'Of course. Shall I fill yours?'

'No, thanks. I'll do mine later. I'll read for a while.'

She filled her bottle. 'Goodnight,' she said.

'Goodnight, Siana. Sleep well.'

She went out, up into her room, undressed, washed and got into bed. There was no lock on her door, and even if there were, that wouldn't stop him. She snuggled into bed and hugged the bottle, determined to stay wide awake, waiting, unsure, apprehensive—yet excited at the same time. She closed her eyes and prepared to wait, to see. . . .

When she awoke it was nearly seven-thirty, and she was alone. Slowly she sat up in bed and looked around as if Matthew might be hiding. She was alone, her door was still closed, and she was safe. Why then, as she lay back in bed, did she feel the faintest sense of something approaching dismay?

The air was cold, she was snug. The temptation to have another hour in bed was too great to resist and Siana didn't even try. She slid down and pulled the covers up. Ah, that was good, so comfortable, so warm. She drifted off into a pleasant half sleep in which plans for the day became muddled with games of chess on a board that filled the entire hall. . . .

There was a tap on the door, Matthew's voice: 'Siana, I've brought you a cup of tea.'

'Come in.' Why had he bothered to knock? she thought wryly. He came in carrying a tray with cup of tea and plate of toast and marmalade. She sat up and looked at it, pulling on her dressing gown as she did so. 'Toast?' she gasped. *'Toast?'*

'Hmm, don't think it's a miracle till you try it.' He sat on the end of the bed and watched her take the first crunchy bite. She looked at him.

'It's good—it's different—it's——' she searched for a word.

'Soda bread,' he finished for her. 'I made some last night after you'd gone to bed.'

'It's smashing!'

'Glad you like it. I'll leave you to it. It's warm downstairs, snow's deeper than ever outside, news

on the radio just as depressing as yesterday, and
we have work to do, so I suggest you get up when
you've finished your tea.'

He had a concise way of delivering the news, and
she smiled, then said thoughtfully: 'Work? In the
house?'

'Yes and no. Not physical work—but certainly in
the house. No one but a madman would go out in
this.' He stood up.

'Wait—what *do* you mean?'

'You'll see.' Then she knew.

'It's about me, isn't it? I mean, it's going to be
something following on from the chess?'

'Right in one. Have you ever been hypnotised?'

Alarm flared. '*No!*' She looked at him. 'You're
not——'

He began to walk away. 'You'll see.'

'No, wait—Matthew, don't leave me like that.
I've no intention of being hypnotised. It's dangerous.'

'In the wrong hands, yes, I agree. And if you
don't want to be hypnotised, then you won't be. I
certainly wouldn't attempt it against your wishes,
even if that were possible. But we'll talk first——'

'I'm staying here!'

He smiled. 'Are you? All day? What are you
scared of?'

'You.' She needed that cup of tea now. She drank
it quickly. 'You're a photographer, not a doctor——'

'Siana, my father was a doctor, and more. He was
a psychiatrist who practised hypno-therapy. Do you
know what that means?'

'I'm not sure.'

'You will. He taught me practically all he knew about hypnosis and its uses in medicine, in qualified hands. That was what I meant when I first met you and told you I could help you. You weren't ready for anything so complex then, but you are now.'

She was suddenly frightened, and Matthew saw, and his face softened fractionally. 'You'll be quite safe, I promise you.'

'How do I know?'

'Because I've said so, that's how.' He walked quietly out of the bedroom and left her feeling as if the world was tilting crazily. She finished the toast and put the tray on the floor. No, she wasn't going to allow it. He had said he wouldn't do it against her will, and that it was impossible anyway.... The thoughts whirled chaotically round in her head; the surge of hope during the chess game, when memory had released some small part of previous knowledge, Matthew's sure confident manner, the complete authority in his voice when he spoke....

She had to get up, if only because she felt at a disadvantage in bed. She found her slippers and put them on, then went to wash.

They sat by a roasting fire and Matthew explained how everything worked in hypnosis, how controlled everything was, how it had helped people in mental illness, and despite her inner misgivings and fears, Siana found it fascinating to listen to. At one point he said in an abrupt change of subject: 'Was it never suggested that you should be hypnotised, Siana?'

She tried to remember. There had been something, but it was difficult to think of that time after hospital with any clarity. 'I think—I've an idea Uncle Peter said he didn't want anything to do with it——' She stopped, realising something, and he nodded.

'I wonder why?'

'He's very old-fashioned.'

'You think that was the reason?'

'It—it must have been——' She hesitated, sensing something in his tone. 'What do you think? Why do you say it like that?'

He shrugged. 'Has it ever occurred to you that they prefer you as you are, not remembering?'

'But why?'

'I wish I knew.' He looked hard at her.

A shiver ran up her spine, chilling her. 'No,' she said, shaking her head. 'That makes no sense. It can't. They want what's best for me.'

'Do they? Is that why they don't let you mix?'

'I don't know. You're confusing me.' She put her hand to her head.

'All right—subject closed.' He stood up. 'We'll leave it for now. Have you any wood anywhere?'

'Wood? In the shed outside. What for? The fire?'

'Not that kind of wood.' He smiled. 'I mean for constructing something like skis or snowshoes.'

'Oh. Where are you going?' She had a sudden vision of him going away and leaving her alone, and that thought was unbearable. She looked at him in alarm. He couldn't—he mustn't!

'Relax.' A grin broke out. 'Did you think I was planning to leave?'

'Not at all!' she replied with dignity.

'You little liar.' He sat down again. 'You looked like a frightened rabbit just then. Did you think I was going to say—right, if you won't let me hypnotise you, I'm leaving?'

It was precisely the thought which had crossed her mind. She glared at him. 'You try to confuse me,' she accused.

'That's precisely what I'm not trying to do. I simply want to construct something wearable if it's necessary—if the snow doesn't go away, and it's certainly no use leaving things like that until the minute before you need them. I promise you most solemnly that I have no intention of leaving you here alone, not for any reason. And if it worries you so much then I'll try and find enough wood for us both. Okay?'

Siana nodded. 'You must think I'm an awful idiot.'

'No, I don't. You're reacting in a perfectly natural way in these circumstances. But you must try to be less timid——'

'I'm not!'

'Of course you are! You've been conditioned to it for two years by——'

'Don't say it. You think my aunt and uncle are responsible——'

'I'm damned sure they are. And so are you, now.'

'Only because you put the doubts in my mind,' she sparked back. 'I was perfectly happy before you came on the scene!'

'Happy? Oh, come on, Siana, you call that existence, permanently half doped, happiness? You can do better than that.'

She stood up, too agitated to remain sitting down. 'There you go again.'

He stood up as well, and they faced each other, only a foot or so apart, she bristling with anger, he calm, which perversely maddened her more. 'You think you know it all!' she snapped crossly, resisting the impulse to stamp her foot. 'Well, you don't. You don't really know them at all!'

'No, but I'd like to. A right couple of weirdos if you ask me——'

'I don't ask you!' she stormed. 'How dare you call them weirdos—that's a disgusting word!'

'I bet you don't even know what it means.'

'I can guess. Don't treat me as though I'm *stupid*, Matthew Craven, just because you think you're so *clever*——'

'That's it, lose your temper—that doesn't get you anywhere——'

'I'll do what I *want*, thank you!' she shouted, infuriated by his calm. 'Don't tell me what to do— you don't own me, you know.'

'Nor do they. But you've let them——'

'Oh, go to hell! Go and find your own wood and as far as I'm concerned, you can buzz off home and stay there. See if I care!'

Matthew began to laugh, and that was the last

straw. She launched herself at him, pummelling his chest with upraised fists. He caught hold of her and held her off, and she struggled impotently, furiously.

'Let me *go*!'

'And get myself beaten up by a little wildcat? No thanks, I'm not that stupid either.' He was still laughing and she kicked him on the shin.

'Ouch, you little bitch,' he grated. 'Do that again and I'll give you a damned good spanking!'

'You wouldn't *dare*!' she spat.

'Wouldn't I just? You'll find out if you do——' She kicked him again, hard, and he winced with pain, grabbed her, twisted her round. and pulled her down with him on to the chair. Helpless, kicking uselessly, she was held face down over his knee.

'Right, you asked for this,' he grated.

'Ouch! Let me go—aaah!' She cried out as his palm descended in a hard slap on her bottom, then again.

'Are you going to behave like a civilised creature?' he asked.

'No! You're a beast. A *beast*—you——'

Wallop! The third slap was satisfyingly hard, then he pulled her to her feet and held her. 'And I'll do it again,' he said.

Siana was crying with humiliation more than pain, sobbing helplessly, and now thoroughly chastened. She stood there limply and Matthew took her and pushed her down, not ungently, into her chair, then stood towering over her. He was breathing hard, as though he had been running.

'Boy, have you got a temper,' he said.

'Go away,' she sobbed. 'I hate you!'

'No, you don't' He pulled her to her feet, and did something totally unexpected. He put his arms round her and held her to him. Nothing violent in it, he held her firmly but gently, and whispered in her ear, 'I'm sorry, Siana, but I had to do it. It was for a reason.'

Her muffled sobs subsided. Alarmingly, she found the fact that he was now holding her so closely after his brutal treatment not at all distressing. It was almost as if she should be just there. She took a deep shuddering breath and said, puzzled: 'What do you mean?'

'Don't you know?' he asked softly. 'I did it on purpose—provoked you into lashing out——'

She tried to push him away. 'On purpose? How—how *could* you?'

He stroked her hair. His touch soothed her, it was very gentle. 'To see something. And now I have.'

'Can I share the joke?' She didn't mind any more, because in some strange way she knew what he was going to say.

'It was no joke. Very far from it, it was deadly serious. Listen to me carefully. What I'm going to say may surprise you, may even shock you, but just listen, and then see what you have to say.' Still he held her, and she was so safe in those arms, and there was nothing remotely sexual in the embrace, it was like a kindly doctor soothing her, which was most odd, because Matthew didn't look remotely like a doctor, and he was very much all male, an aggressive sexual animal.

'You are normal, very normal and sane, Siana, and there's no reason in the world why you shouldn't get your memory back fully. I provoked you into argument quite cold-bloodedly and deliberately to see what your reaction would be—and boy, I sure found out.' He squeezed her tightly for a moment. 'You're sane and sensible—a bit fiery-tempered, but nothing much wrong with that—and your reactions to my provocation were what I'd hoped for. If that makes me sound cruel, I apologise. But I had to know if you'd got those damned pills out of your system for good. You have. Now do you understand?'

'Yes,' she said quietly, because it was what she had known. 'I think I need a drink. I feel as though I've just been through the wringer!'

'Sit down. In a way you've been through something far more drastic. I'll make us a cup of coffee. You do realise that I'll probably have a beautiful couple of bruises on my leg, don't you?'

'I'm sorry,' she said. He released her.

'I'll live. I walloped you, don't forget.'

'I can hardly forget that. I really *hated* you then.'

'I know—I felt the waves of aggression. That too was necessary.' He grinned 'Now the air's cleared, are you ready for the treatment after lunch?'

'I don't know.' She shook her head. 'I'll have to think about it. Let me recover from one shock before you give me another.' She sat down and said: 'Ouch!'

'It hurts?'

'It hurts.' She looked at him. 'I'll bet you enjoyed it,' she said accusingly.

Matthew laughed as he turned away, but he didn't answer her. She watched him filling the kettle. What a strange, unpredictable, powerful man he was! There were depths to him that she couldn't even have begun to suspect, facets to his personality quite beyond her imagining. She had just seen one other aspect of him. And there were more, she was certain of that. Highly complex, deeply intelligent— she already knew that, but she began now to think he was possibly of a far greater intelligence than she had thought. She recalled their first meeting on the beach, the one he had admitted he had 'engineered'. And he had watched her before, from a distance, sometimes through binoculars—enough to do a detailed and very accurate painting, as yet unfinished. It made it seem as if he were a force who had entered her life inevitably—as if he had intended it to happen and waited his moment. The big unanswered question she couldn't even begin to ask him was, why? Why me? she thought. And now he has changed my life in other ways too, one more important and devastating than the rest. She remembered that all right. She would never, ever, forget. He looked round at that moment, as if he could sense her thoughts, and she hastily blanked them out, picked a book from the top of the pile beside her chair and looked at it. It would be the one she had intended never to touch again, the one on amnesia.

'That's good,' he said. 'I wondered when you'd get round to reading it.'

'I'm not—I just——' It seemed foolish to put it down. He could well wonder why, in that case, she had troubled to pick it up in the first place. She opened it at random and glanced casually, her eyes skimming the page, intending to close it after a moment or two and suggest finding that wood— only she was caught by the opening sentence of a paragraph, clearly on a case history. 'Mrs M. had been knocked out by a falling beam, when the house she lived in with her family was bombed in 1941. Miraculously the others were unhurt, or received only minor injuries. In hospital it was discovered that she had severe concussion and a suspected fractured skull, but it wasn't until her husband visited her and she failed to recognise him that it was realised she had amnesia. Naturally enough, the doctors reassured Mr M. that the condition was temporary. It was quite common in wartime, the subconscious desire perhaps to blot out the horrors that daily surrounded normal citizens. But in her case it turned out to be more severe, and when she was discharged from hospital several days later, unavoidably owing to the extreme shortage of beds, she was still totally without any recall of her life previous to the night of the bomb.'

Siana looked up at Matthew. 'Is it full of case histories?' she asked him.

'There is a chapter on them, yes.' He turned away to make the coffee and, she couldn't help it, she continued to read. She didn't want to—but she did. She began to wonder if, by chance, she had picked on the one case that seemed to apply equally to herself, or if they were all like that. And there was only one way to find out. Matthew was very quietly busy at the sink, but she was scarcely aware of his presence.

The anonymous Mrs M. had had to make a life among what—to her—were complete strangers. She had attended the outpatients department for several months afterwards, but owing to the intense pressure on nursing staff her treatment had been, of necessity, cursory. Physically, she was healthy. Mentally she was not, but there seemed nothing to be done. Four years later, on holiday at the end of the war at a country farm of relatives, she had been walking across a cobbled yard, slippery with rain and spilt hay, fallen and broken her leg. The shock had done what medical treatment had failed to do, and she had recognised the 'strangers' she had come to accept as her family, for the first time in four years. 'It was like being born again,' she was quoted as saying. 'I remembered everything. It was wonderful. It had been like being only half alive during that time.' Siana looked up again. The woman had described her own feelings exactly. Tears filled her eyes, and Matthew saw, and said:

'Don't read if it upsets you.'

'It doesn't. I'm glad you brought it. I would like to read it, but not all at once.' She held the book out. 'A bit at a time will do, I think.'

'Okay. As you wish.' He shrugged. 'Let's have our coffee.' He handed her a steaming beaker.

'It's a bit drastic.' She tapped the page. 'I mean, I hope I don't have to break a leg——'

'Oh, that one! No, that was just one example. There are others, describing the therapy—you'll see for yourself anyway. There's all the time in the world, Siana.'

She looked at him, half amused, yet disturbed at the same time. 'All the time in the world?'

'Oh yes,' he answered softly. 'But you already know that, don't you?'

'I'm sorry, I don't follow.' She shook her head. There was something in his words, something in the way he said them that was almost frightening— yet not.

She saw a muscle tighten in his jaw. His face was suddenly quite serious. 'When they come back— when the snows have gone—it won't just end there.'

'What—what do you mean?' She caught her breath.

'You know what I mean. Even if, in three weeks, you still have no memory of where you were before, there can be no going back to the person you were, to that sedated childlike waif I saw on the beach. It will continue——'

She was unable to move, caught by the power in his words, looking into his eyes and seeing the dark, unfathomable depths to him, aware only of him. 'Continue,' she echoed softly.

'They can't stop me seeing you. Even if they want to they won't be able to. They'd have to lock you up, and they wouldn't dare do that—and you will come to my house——' his voice had changed, it had become very soothing and quiet, 'you will come there every day and we'll sit and talk. You'd like that, wouldn't you, Siana?'

'Yes, I suppose so.'

He was fingering the silver St Christopher he always wore round his neck as he spoke. She watched it, fascinated. 'It will be quite easy, even if there is more snow—for then I would come here, and we can sit here or in another warm room out of anyone's way, and perhaps I'll continue to do the painting of you. It's very soothing to paint, you know. Gently stroking the brush on to the canvas, backwards and forwards, slowly, slowly——' he moved his fingers, the ones that held the medallion, softly back and forth as if in time with an imaginary brush and it seemed very sensible and soothing to her and quite beautiful to watch. She could almost see the brush on the canvas, and she didn't want to speak and he didn't seem to expect her to, and the medallion caught the light and gleamed and seemed to grow larger, which was her imagination but it didn't seem important anyway. It seemed to be filling the entire room now and she couldn't see anything else except perhaps his eyes and the shadowed blur of his face. She was perfectly relaxed and in a minute she would have her coffee before it got cold.

'——and the painting grows, like this medallion, it grows bigger and bigger and moves left to right, forwards and back, forwards and back, and your eyes grow heavier and heavier and you're very tired and sleepy and comfortable and you're going to sleep now when I count to ten—one—two—three——' his voice grew fainter, far away, now from a great distance, now so faint that she could scarcely hear it——

'And now I want you to wake up, Siana.'

She opened her eyes, and looked round for her coffee, blinked and yawned. 'Good grief, what happened? Don't tell me I've been asleep?'

Matthew smiled. 'I'd better make another cup. That one's cold.'

'How can it be? You only made it two minutes ago. What were we talking about? I feel as though I've just woken up.'

'You have. And it wasn't two minutes ago I made it, it was sixty. You Siana, have just been on a trip into the past—and very interesting it was too.'

She stared blankly at him, then smiled as if humouring a child. 'You'll be telling me next that you just hypnotised me!'

'I did.'

'But—you can't have—you said you couldn't, unless I wanted——'

'I know. Normally you can't—but you were receptive—it just happened. We were talking about what would happen when your aunt and uncle returned, I was telling you how we'd keep on visiting regardless of whether they wanted it or not, you were listening, and suddenly I knew that this was the moment. You were relaxed, receptive, listening—and I went ahead. It didn't hurt, did it?'

She shook her head, vague memories of a conversation surfacing, then—nothing. Yet she felt splendid. 'And that's it?' she asked. 'You talk—oh yes, you had your medallion—you were holding it, weren't you, and talking about painting—I remember that.' She frowned. 'It grew larger and larger. It filled the room!'

He nodded. 'And do you remember anything after that?'

'No. You asked me questions?'

'Yes. I took you back to when you were sixteen.'

'What did I say? Did I—did I remember anything?'

'Quite a lot. In a minute I'll tell you everything. But first, a fresh coffee and something to eat. You've just been on a long journey, Siana.'

A long journey. That was what he had said. She suddenly knew there was hope, and a surge of excitement coursed through her blood. She waited in a fever of impatience to hear what he had to say. And perhaps, when he told her, she herself would truly remember.

CHAPTER-SEVEN

It was like hearing someone's life story. Fascinating, because it was her own, but still it was like someone else's life. As yet she felt no personal connection with what Matthew was telling her. But he reassured her that it was fairly normal, and at some point, perhaps in days—or weeks—something would 'click' and the true memory would begin to flood back. Siana held on to that reassurance like a magic talisman, and listened. He had only taken her a journey of several months in that first hour-long session, he said. And there were eight more years to go to bring her up to the present.

She asked, impatiently, when he had finished: 'When can we have another try?'

'Not today.' He smiled. 'Don't rush it. You've a lot to catch up on—and I told you, we have the time.'

'Yes, of course.' At sixteen she had been living with her mother and father in Manchester, still at school, and clearly a star pupil. She had recalled the names of several friends, the youth club she went to, the name of their pet dog, a spaniel. As Matthew filled in the missing details of a life she had already had sketched in by her aunt and uncle, it was like seeing the colours being washed on to a black and white picture. They had known basic details, naturally enough; Matthew was providing the breath of life—and it was because she herself knew it subconsciously.

He had made notes on a writing pad, and when their conversation ended he tapped it and said: 'That will be full when we've done—and then you'll be yourself again.'

'A whole person,' she said wryly.

'You are now.' He smiled. 'All it needs is bringing out. Now, the wood, and then lunch.'

'And after lunch?'

'Painting. My fingers are itching to get back to that picture.'

'Of course. But you've no easel.'

'I'll find something, don't worry. Now, I'm going out to the shed—if I can fight my way through.'

'Be careful.'

He looked at her, smiled drily. 'It's only about ten yards.'

'I know, but——'

'No buts. You can watch me flounder through the snow and have a good laugh. Let me get my coat and boots on.'

He found them and sat down to put his wellingtons on, and Siana went to the door and opened it. It seemed totally impassable. A few errant snowflakes drifted down to vanish into the crystal shimmering crisp surface that was nearly up to her shoulders. She thought, with feeling, I'm glad I'm not alone. She would have been terrified. Yet with him there, the snow didn't seem threatening at all.

He stood behind her, she was aware of his solid

physical presence close to her before he even spoke.
'Wish me luck.'

'Don't forget—it's two steps down.'

'Thanks for reminding me.' He stepped out, and
down, and turned, laughing, breast high in the
white solid mass, making swimming motions with
his arms. 'Goodbye—•—' he let his voice tail off,
as if he were distant already, and Siana bit her lip,
knowing she should be amused, but too full of
apprehension to appreciate the humour. Her nails
were digging into her palms, and she was cold, and
she didn't want to let him out of her sight. Then
he had disappeared round the wall of the house,
leaving only the broken trail through the snow.
Silence fell. The air was diamond-bright, almost
hurtful to the eyes, and high up two gulls wheeled
and swooped in a grey heavy sky. Siana put her
coat on and stood waiting for what seemed an eternity.

Then she heard him call her name, and he re-
appeared, a tall dark figure, only the top half of
him visible as yet, bearing aloft a pile of wood—
and her heart leapt, and in that instant of time she
knew that she had fallen in love with him. A sob
escaped her, and warmth flooded through her at
the realisation of something so new and startling
that it was almost frightening. She knew, she had
known for a day or so, that she was to him merely
a body to use—and a mind that was a challenge
to his brain. It didn't seem to matter at that moment.
All that mattered was what she knew. And with her
new knowledge came another more disturbing

thought. What if he found out things about her of which she was ashamed? She knew nothing of herself—he was going to.

His voice broke into her thoughts. 'Found some.' He was closer now, 'Good grief, it's like fighting through a jungle, a white solid jungle.' He came the last few steps, kicked the snow off his wellingtons, and began to shake himself to rid his coat and trousers of the clinging snow.

'Let me help.' She took the wood from him and put it down, then began to brush with her hands at his shoulders and arms. She wanted to touch his face, to warm his frozen cheeks with her hands. The temptation was almost irresistible, and she drew back, lest he see.

'Phew!' He was in then, kicking off the heavy wellingtons, putting on the espadrilles he had brought, and Siana took his coat and hung it on the door hook.

'Is it really that bad?'

'It is.' He was about to say more when the telephone shrilled in the hall. He looked at her, raised an eyebrow quizzically, and said: 'That's a bit early for them, isn't it?'

'Yes.' She ran to answer it.

But it wasn't her aunt, it was Mrs Patterson from the village store calling to see if Siana was all right. Her voice came over the line very faint and crackly almost as if she were calling from a great distance instead of a mere mile or so, but the concern was genuine, and clear enough. 'Och it's me, Siana, Molly Patterson. We were so worried about you being alone in that big house just now.'

'I've got a friend staying with me,' Siana answered, before she realised what she was saying. It seemed more important to reassure the kindly woman whose anxiety was real.

'Och, that's fine. We're so snowed up here, no one can get out of their doors. It's just terrible. But as long as you're not alone, that's a relief.'

'No, I'm fine, thank you for asking, and there's plenty of food. The snow won't last for ever—though it seems pretty permanent at the moment. My only worry is that my aunt won't be able to phone if the lines go down, but I've already told her that could happen, and she knows what it's like from the news.'

'Aye, and you're keeping warm, then?'

'Oh yes. It's very kind of you to ring, Mrs Patterson. I appreciate it.'

'Och, I'm calling all my customers who're too far from the village to check up that they're safe. With us being the post office, you see, I'm keeping in touch with the authorities. It keeps a link going with everyone. Thank the lord for telephones, I say! Mr Craven now is not on the phone, so there's no way we can contact him, but—well, he's a strong young fellow, I'm sure he'll be managing.'

'He—managed to get through to here, actually, Mrs Patterson to see if I—we—were safe——' she hated lying, and was stammering, but it was only fair to reassure the kindly woman, and it certainly wouldn't do to have a search party going to his cottage to find it closed and empty. 'He's here at the moment—er—having a cup of tea.' That wasn't a lie. She had heard the kettle, and the clatter of crockery from the kitchen.

'There's a relief! Well, tell him I was asking. It would make sense if he stayed on. I've always thought Marine Cottage is a cold place in winter— but there, it's no business of mine! Well, I'll go now, dear. I have to try and get through to old Mr and Mrs Menzies at Duthie Farm.'

'Yes. Thank you, Mrs Patterson. I'll see you when the snow's over. Goodbye.'

'Goodbye just now.' The line clicked and went dead, and Siana went in to tell the waiting man about Mrs Patterson's suggestion. He had already gathered most of what she had said from Siana's remarks, and he looked at her and smiled slightly.

'I wonder who she thinks you have staying here officially?'

'I just said a friend. It seemed to ease her mind. I don't like telling fibs.'

'I could tell that from your voice. It was a necessary lie, Siana, don't forget. This is an emergency situation, remember. Sit down and have your coffee—not tea. Then we'd better eat, I'm starving.'

'Can you do anything with the wood?'

'I'm going to have a try. Your uncle's tool box is here somewhere, isn't it?'

'Yes. I'll get it afterwards.' She sank into the fireside chair and put her head back. 'Oh, I'm so tired!'

'You've been through quite a time, being hypnotised. Relax. There's no hurry for anything, and you're not going anywhere, so close your eyes for a few minutes.'

Not going anywhere, he said. But she was. 'I'm going back into the past,' she said softly. 'That is somewhere—for me. Somewhere new and strange. Even though it doesn't mean anything personally to me yet, I know it will.' She looked at him. And I'm going with you on this journey, she thought, and now I know that I love you, I wonder about it, about why you're doing it, and even if I asked I doubt if I'd find the truth. She wanted him to touch her, to take her in his arms again. She ached for him in a way she found disturbing and new, and warmth flooded her at certain memories and she moved uneasily in the chair and turned to the fire so that he would not see her face. She was ashamed of her thoughts and half understood longings. Aunt Peggy was kind, but very narrow-minded. If there was a play on television that was even mildly sexy, the set was turned off, or over. They treat me like a child, she thought, and I'm twenty-four, I'm a woman. And there's no one I can talk to——

'What is it?' he said softly.

'Nothing.' But then she began to cry.

'Oh, Siana, for heaven's sake child, tell me.' Child, he called her. Perhaps he regarded her as one as well—mentally anyway. She fumbled for her handkerchief.

'Just leave me alone—please.' The pent-up emotion of two years was too much for her. Sobs racked her body and when she felt his hand on her arm, she pushed him away. 'No—you don't understand, no one does—it's me—there's something wrong with me—don't, don't you see——'

'There's nothing wrong with you.' He lifted her to her feet like the child she felt she had become, and put his arms round her.

'Don't cry, Siana. Is it my fault?'

Of course it's your fault, she wanted to cry. Don't you know what you've done? She felt revulsion, sudden overwhelming dislike for him, for what he was doing, and struggled impotently in his arms. 'Let me go—you don't understand——'

'When you stop crying I'll let you go.' He lifted her chin up with his free hand. 'Look at me.'

She resolutely closed her eyes and shook her head. 'No—no, you——'

'I understand. I understand only too well.' His tone was soothing—she hated him. She wriggled her body and pushed at his chest, but vainly. He laughed very softly. 'I'm not going to let you go. Not while you're like this.'

She knew he meant precisely what he said, and she was too weak to resist, and in any case her struggles were having a disturbing effect on her— and apparently on him, and she wasn't sure now if she knew what she was doing there, because her mind was getting totally confused and filled with a warmth that was suffusing her body, her wretched, treacherous body as well, and the awful thing, the worst thing of all, was that he knew it too.

He pulled her closer to him, bent his head, and

kissed her aching eyes, then her nose, and lastly her mouth. It was a warm, gentle, undemanding kiss, and his stubble prickled her cheeks, and she didn't care any more. She responded to the kiss like a flower to the sun, then it was suddenly not gentle, but harder, more demanding, and his lips were on her chin, her throat; she arched her head back, revelling in the warmth of him, and the strong caressing expert hands that teased her body and inflamed her senses, and the tears had gone now. Shyly, almost without her being aware of what she was doing, put up her hands to his face, and he looked down at her, his eyes very dark and intense, and she felt as if she would drown in their depths. Her own eyes widened, and she knew he saw what was in them, and gave a little cry.

'Let—me—go——' she whispered.

'You don't want me to,' he answered softly. 'You're very tired, I think you ought to go and lie down for a while,' and he traced his finger down her cheek, smoothing away the last errant tear. She began to shiver, and as she would have answered, he picked her up. She had to keep her arms round his neck then, for fear of falling.

'No, Matthew, put me down——' she said, a token protest, for he was already walking out of the kitchen and into the hall.

'Yes, soon I will. Close your eyes.' She couldn't fight him, but did she want to?

He went into his bedroom and kicked the door closed behind him and she said: 'This isn't my——'

'The bed's bigger,' he said. 'You'll rest better,'

and laid her down after pulling the covers back.
Then he kicked off his sandals and lay beside her.

'You're cold,' he said. 'See how cold it is in here.
You need keeping warm.'

'No, I don't,' her teeth began to chatter. 'I—
you—mustn't——'

He silenced her very effectively with his mouth,
then spoke huskily. 'What mustn't I do?' His hands
began a lazy trail. 'This? Or this?'

She was weakening fast, her own treacherous
responses betraying her. 'You—please don't——'

'There, you mean? Or—there——'

She gasped, the colour in her face betraying
her. 'Matthew—it's wrong, you know it's—we
shouldn't——'

'Shouldn't make love?' he whispered. 'When it's
the most wonderful thing in the world and we both
want to?'

'I don't——'

'Oh, but you do.' His voice was thick and husky.
'I can tell how much you want it.'

'You're mistaken.' She tried to push his hand
away and he obligingly moved it, but only to
another place equally disturbing, then he leaned
slightly away and began to ease up her sweater. He
had her imprisoned with his hard muscular legs,
and she could scarcely move to stop him, and to her
horror, no longer wanted to. Then, suddenly, his
lazy teasing of her was over, and his breathing
changed, became harsh and ragged, and his hands
brooked no resistance, and she was carried along,
unable to resist, not wanting to, helping him, caught

in a wave of passion and excitement that overwhelmed them both in a consuming fire. He whispered the words of love she needed to hear and his body was hard and demanding, she soft, yielding to the overwhelming force of the mounting excitement that consumed them both, carrying them along, inevitable, timeless, lasting for ever, and ever——

Siana slept, and when she awoke she was alone. She didn't want to go down and face Matthew. She wanted to die. He knew now. He knew her, and he knew everything about her, including, most of all, that she was wanton. She pulled the warm covers over her, visualising his face when he should see her. Mocking—satisfied—knowing....

'Siana? Are you awake? Lunch is ready.' He spoke, shouting up the stairs as though everything was perfectly normal. Perhaps, to him, it was. Perhaps he made love to every woman he met. She didn't answer and a moment later heard his footsteps on the stairs.

'Go away,' she whispered fiercely, but he was in the room, and looking at her.

'It's ready to eat.' He sat on the bed and his eyes were upon her, searching, and he wasn't smiling, not quite, but she hated him and she hated herself.

'I'm staying here.'

'No, you're not. Come on.'

'Leave me *alone*!' She grabbed the covers and pulled them up to her chin. 'I hate you!'

He stood up. 'You're coming down now to eat. You don't eat enough, God knows how you stay alive, so stop behaving like a child——'

'Don't keep saying that! I'm not a child——'

'Then stop acting like one.' He flung her clothes from the chair on to the bed. 'Do you want me to dress you?'

'You've done enough, thanks!' She turned her head away. 'She was right—you're all the same.'

'Who was? Don't tell me, let me guess. Our dear Aunt Peggy? Right? And she told you all men are the same—beast I suppose was the word she'd use. Or was it animals? Wanting only one thing?'

'And she was right,' said Siana, choked with impotent rage.

'Yet she's married? Poor Uncle Peter——'

'Leave him out of it! He's not like——' she faltered.

'Not like me? I'll bet he's not, poor devil. This household sounds more weird the more I hear about it. The sooner you get out of here, the better. They'll have you as crazy as they are in a few years——'

She sat up, forgetting her nakedness, and hastily grabbed her sweater and fumbled to put it on. 'It's not they who're mad, it's you,' she said.

'You're forgetting your bra.'

'Oh, go to hell!' She glared at him. 'Turn away.'

He did so and she dressed in record time and slid out of the bed. She tried to walk past him but he caught her arm. 'They're wrong, you know they are, yet you deny it even when you hear me speak the truth. Why?'

She tried to shake herself free. 'You use *me*, don't deny it. I despise you—you think you only have to kiss me——' she was beginning to tremble with cold and temper, 'and I'll fall into your arms. I suppose this is how you treat all women——'

'No, I don't. I don't go around raping them, if that's what you mean.'

'You could have fooled me!' She managed to free her arm and walked out. He made no attempt to stop her but followed her in silence to the kitchen. 'I don't want you to touch me again,' she said.

'All right, I won't.' He seemed very calm.

'Huh! You say that now,' she gasped. 'That's easy enough to say—until the next time——'

'There won't be a next time,' he cut in.

'And what about when you hypnotise me? You can——'

'Can what? Force you to submit? You've been watching too many films, Siana. You can't be made to do anything under hypnosis that you don't want to do——'

'I don't believe you. You're a liar!'

'Then you have the solution. I won't hypnotise you again.'

She stared at him unbelieving. 'But you——'

'No,' he said softly. 'I don't think you really want to find out about yourself. I think you're scared. That's okay by me, if that's what you want. Stay here with them. Live here until you die, just go on existing here like you have been—if you ask them nicely I'm sure they'll get you some pretty "pills" you can take to keep you pleasantly doped—and you'll get older and older, and life will pass you by, but you'll be safe. That's probably why you chose to lose your memory in the first place, because you're too scared to face up to living. You're a coward, Siana, do you hear me or shall I spell it out? A coward——'

'No!' she screamed, and hit him hard. He caught her and pulled her towards him.

'The no touching rule works two ways, Siana. I don't touch you and you don't touch me—and that includes slapping my face because you don't like what I'm saying. So let's get that straight right now. We'll behave like civilised human beings.' He let her go and pushed her slightly from him. His eyes gleamed darkly and she had never seen him look so powerful—or so angry. She was suddenly frightened of the strength and force of him, and backed towards a chair and put her hand on the back of it. She felt as if her world was crumbling. Her new-found safety—with him—the strength he gave her—all being taken from her. She didn't want him to be angry, but it was too late for that.

Hard-eyed, like a stranger, not the same man who only an hour or so before had held her and taken her into a world she had never known, he stood there facing her, relentless, his words coming at her, and no way to stop them or to stop listening to them. 'It's your choice now. I've finished. You don't want me to help you, do you? You should never have let them leave you alone here. You say I must stop calling you a child, but that's how you are. So be it. They'll be back in just over two weeks and your life can go on the same as it's always been and always will be. I hope I'm making myself clear, because I don't intend to repeat myself. And if and when we should meet on the beach at any time. I'll say good morning or good afternoon, but that will be all. I shall not attempt to make conversation with you or in any way force my attention on you.' He turned away. 'I've said all that I'm going to. I'll serve up lunch and then I shall see what I can make with the wood. I'm not going to paint the picture of you any more, I don't wish to.'

Numbly, shattered beyond all belief by his terrible words, Siana went to sit at the table. Her head and throat ached with the effort not to cry, and she had never felt so wretched and unhappy before. Matthew meant every word he said, and he was harsh and cruel, but somehow there had been a devastating justice in all he had said.

They ate in silence, he reading a book, she finding it an effort to swallow anything. The food tasted like cardboard in her dry mouth, but she forced herself to finish it lest he scourge her with more scorn. At last, mercifully, it was over. She went and washed the dishes, and still not a word had been said.

Then he stood up. 'I'll work in the laundry room,' he said, picking up his wood.

'But it's freezing along that passage——'

'I'll wear my coat.' He picked that up and walked out of the small door that led to the coal store and laundry room. Siana watched him go. It was as though he were walking out of her life. There was something symbolic in his going there to work. Because he didn't want to be in the same room as her. He must despise her, feel only a huge contempt for her and all she had become. She stood by the table and the memory and force of his words came back to her, sweeping through her, leaving her spent and exhausted. For she knew the truth of them.

She knew too that she had reached rock bottom. She could stay there, accepting his words, accepting that when her aunt and uncle returned she could slide back into the easy way of non-resistance—or she could begin to climb out. And if she left it any longer it would be too late. If the atmosphere that filled the house were not destroyed now, then she would be destroyed herself, and she would never escape.

She began to breathe quietly and deeply, forcing herself to calmness, seeking and praying inwardly for some kind of strength to enable her to take the first steps on the road to sanity and self respect.

He was angry with her, perhaps justifiably so. But she was not going to grovel. She was not going to lose her temper, or strike him ever again. She was going to stop behaving like the child he regarded her. And gradually as the minutes passed, the inner pleas for help were answered. A sense of quiet filled her, her breathing became steadier, a kind of inward calm became a part of her.

She was twenty-four, an adult woman, with an adult mind. Her thoughts were her own. She belonged to herself, not to the two people who, rightly or wrongly, had run her life for two long years. She belonged completely to herself, not to Matthew Craven. She was now going to meet him, and talk to him, on those terms.

She went across and looked into the mirror over the fireplace. Her face looked back at her and she saw the new resolution reflected in the glass, in her eyes. She smoothed her hair back from her face, took a deep breath and went out of the door, into the corridor from where she could hear the sounds of hammering.

She paused in the doorway of the laundry room to see him kneeling hammering nails into the wood. 'Matthew,' she said. He paused and looked up, then, slowly rose to his feet.

'Yes?'

'May I speak with you—now, in the kitchen?'

'Haven't we said it all?' Hard-faced, hard-eyed, unyielding.

She shook her head and smiled very slightly. 'No. There's more, much more. You were right in everything you said. And I've been thinking about your words, and knowing the truth of them. You've opened my eyes at last, and I wanted you to know it.' She stood tall and calm and straight, facing him, and she felt strong, as strong as he, and she knew what she had to say. 'I would like to talk to you, in the kitchen where it's warmer, if possible, but if not, here will do. Whichever you choose.'

He put down the hammer. He hadn't once taken his eyes off her. 'You're different,' he said. 'Something's changed you.'

'I know. I just discovered I'm no longer a child. I thought you should be the first to know.'

'We'll talk in the kitchen.' She turned and walked out, and as he followed her she thought he said something. It was so faint she wasn't even sure if she was right, but it sounded like: 'Thank God— at last.'

CHAPTER EIGHT

SHE waited until he had closed the door. 'Won't you sit down?' she asked politely, as though he was a casual visitor calling for tea.

'Are you going to?'

She shook her head. 'Then I'll stand as well,' he said. They were facing each other, near the fire where it was warm. Siana lifted her chin.

'I hated you for what you were saying, but it was the best thing you could have done. I saw very clearly how right you were, and I want to say I'm sorry for behaving as I did. It won't happen again. I do truly want to regain my memory, and I will also tell you that after my aunt and uncle return I shall leave this house. You're right about them as well. Perhaps not in everything, but certainly in the essentials. I've done a lot of growing up in this last half hour or so. I don't intend to go back to what I was before.' She paused. He was silent. Before, he had done all the talking. Now, it seemed, it was Siana's turn.

'I will ask you, just once, if you will continue to help me. If you say no, and I shan't blame you if you do, I won't ask again, I promise.' She paused again. This was the moment. 'Will you hypnotise me again?'

'Yes.'

'Thank you.' She smiled, then continued. 'I'm going to be different from now on. And when Aunt Peggy telephones I shall tell her you're here. I'm not ashamed to tell her that now. I was frightened before. I don't think I'm frightened of anything any more. Thank you for that.' She ran her tongue over lips that had suddenly become dry. 'I think I've said all I want or need to say now. I'm sorry I dragged you from your work, but I had to say it all while it was fresh in my mind.'

He nodded. Still he looked at her as though he couldn't take his eyes from her. 'I'm glad you did. I was brutal to you before—deliberately so. I didn't imagine it would have such an immediate—or devastating effect. You're different.' He smiled slightly. 'I hope your new-found resolve doesn't weaken when your aunt has hysterics over the telephone.'

'It won't, I promise.'

'Good. I think we'll sit down now. There's a lot more to be said—now that at last we really understand one another.' He waited until she was seated, then pulled a kitchen chair by the side of her and sat on it. He was close, but not too close. Close enough to touch if he wanted to. 'It won't be easy, but it'll be a hell of a lot easier than it would have been if we hadn't cleared the air like this. There'll be no more fighting, I can promise you that. Siana, I've got something I'd like you to have. You weren't ready before—but I think this can help you.' He fished in his jacket pocket and found a small box while she watched, puzzled.

He opened it, and inside was an ornate gold ring,

clearly very old and heavy-looking.

He handed it to her. Siana held it carefully. 'It's beautiful, but—what——'

'It has a special significance for me, Siana. Humour me, please. I'd like you to wear it, and when—next time—I hypnotise you I'd like you to hold it.'

'And you think it will help?' She gazed at it fascinated, and it seemed to her as if she had seen it before, which was quite impossible, of course, but it seemed somehow *right*. 'It's—odd——' she said, 'I feel as if——' she paused. He didn't speak, he didn't prompt her, he sat and looked at her. She shook her head. 'It's a beautiful ring, Matthew. I'll wear it, of course—but I'd be frightened of losing it.' Yet she knew she had to have it. She wanted to wear it.

'Then let's see if it fits.' He took it from her and held her right hand. Then he slid it on to the third finger. It might have been made for her. She looked at her hand. It was a round band with no stones, but carved in an intricate design of flowers, of the kind that is often used as a wedding ring. She looked at him.

'It fits perfectly.'

'I hope you'll wear it for——' he seemed to hesitate, 'as long as I'm here.'

'I will. Thank you.' She wasn't sure if she wanted to ask what the special significance was. It might be the answer she didn't want. Yet during that afternoon, as the day darkened into evening, and she busied herself washing lingerie in the bowl, and catching glimpses of the ring as it gleamed softly on her finger, she wondered. Had it belonged to a woman he had loved? He must have made love to many—but to love one would be something special. She tried to imagine what she would have looked like. Tall, small, dark, fair? Matthew was a big man, a powerful man of hardness and intensity yet with flashes of humour and gentleness. A complex mixture—she would not have been an ordinary woman, not for him. He would need someone out of the common run, someone special——

'Did this belong to someone who meant a lot to you, Matthew?' The question Siana hadn't intended to ask—she of the new-found resolve and calm—came out of its own volition as he came up close to her by the clothes airer as she put the clothes on.

He paused, half turned. He had been about to attend to the fire. 'Why do you ask?'

'I shouldn't have—it's none of my business.' She grimaced apologetically at him.

'You're wearing it at my request. That makes it your business.'

'It's such a beautiful ring, that's all. And you said it had some significance.'

'It had—still has. It belonged to the woman I loved dearly.' He looked at Siana. 'It was her wedding ring.'

She swallowed. He had been married. It was something that had simply not occurred to her before. Perhaps he still was. 'You—you were married?'

'Yes.'

'Oh. I'm sorry I asked. You don't mind me wearing it?' She couldn't look at him, not yet. Even her inner new strength hadn't prepared her for this.

'No. I always carry it with me—and it seemed stupid to leave it in the box where it might easily get mislaid when you could wear it.'

'I see.' A perfectly logical explanation. He always carried it with him, which meant one of two things. His wife was dead, or she had left him, returning his ring when she left. Siana didn't want to know which. He must have loved her very much to still carry a ring around with him.

'You're not going to ask me whether I'm still married?'

'No.' She would rather not know if she was an adulteress on top of everything else. She ached inside at the knowledge of his deep love for some unknown woman. That was enough to contend with for the present. 'I'm asking too many questions about you. That's more like the old Siana. This is the new one, remember?'

He laughed. 'There are still touches of the old one that I like. Please don't become too high-minded, I mightn't be able to survive in the rarefied atmosphere.'

'I'll try. But I don't intend asking any personal questions about you. That's one of the new resolutions.'

'So be it. But this evening, after tea, I'm going to take you back and ask you questions. Nothing too complex, more of a simple conversation, but I'll be taking notes. Okay?'

'Yes,' she nodded.

At that moment the telephone rang. Siana looked at Matthew. This was the test. Would she be able to go through with what she planned? She half wished she hadn't said it. Not yet anyway. Because then—then—she might know.

His voice followed her, soft, almost mocking it seemed to her sensitive ears. 'Good luck.'

She picked up the telephone. Her aunt's voice came very distantly, but fairly clearly. 'Hello, Siana, it's me, dear. Is it still as terrible there?'

'Yes. The snow's worse, I'm afraid.'

'But you're keeping well? And warm?'

'Yes, I'm fine. Mrs Patterson phoned. She's calling all those she can to check if they're safe.'

'Yes, well, I suppose she would. You told her you can manage?'

'Yes—I said I'd a friend here—to reassure her.'

'Oh!' That seemed to confuse her aunt slightly. 'B—but what would she think? She knows you don't know anyone. Still, I'll sort it out with her when I get——'

'I have.'

'What did you say, dear? I didn't hear you properly. This line is very strange, I thought you said——'

'I did. I have. It's a neighbour—the man from Marine Cottage.' Her heart was thudding and her mouth was dry.

'A man?' Even with the poor connection Siana could hear the shrillness of her aunt's voice—the shock. 'There's a *man* there? Siana, *what are you saying?*'

'Matthew Craven came over two days ago to see if I was all right——'

'My God!' Siana had never heard Aunt Peggy utter more than a mild 'dash' before. 'He's *staying* there? That horrible stranger——'

'He's not horrible, Aunty. He's been very kind——'

'No! I don't believe it. What are you saying? Siana, have you gone mad?'

'No. The dynamo has broken down—there's no heat——'

'What do you mean, no heat? And what's that got to do with him being there?' Her voice was bordering on hysteria. 'He must leave at once—do you hear? *At once!*'

'He can't, the snow's too——'

'I'm getting your uncle.' She heard her aunt calling his name, as if half turning from the telephone. She wished she had a chair to sit in. Her legs were very wobbly from tension. Even though her aunt's reaction had been expected——

'What's this, Siana?' Her uncle Peter's deeper tones came over the line. 'That man's there? This is impossible, quite impossible—now you're to tell him—I don't know what you're thinking of. We should never have left you, I knew something like this would happen. You're not fit to be left alone,

I said that to Peggy. I should have made you come away with us——'

'I didn't want to. I liked being alone. I didn't know it would snow, and that the dynamo would break down, did I?' Siana was frightened. She had never heard her uncle so angry. His rage was a frightening force, carrying over the miles.

'That's impossible! He's lying to you. It can't——'

'It has, it has,' she said.

'Now listen to me, Siana. Listen carefully. He is to leave that house *now*. I don't care if the snow's eight feet deep, he is to *go*—if he doesn't I'm going to phone the police at Crathmore and tell them you're being held against your will——'

'Don't be ridiculous!' Siana found her voice, and her strength. Their over-reaction to her words was too absurd, and gave her the impetus she needed. 'I'm twenty-four——'

'Put him on at once. *I'll* speak to him. I'll tell him—go and get him.' Siana half turned, and Matthew was there. Hearing, he had approached silently. He looked strong and reassuring.

White-faced, Siana said: 'He wants to speak to you.'

'I'm not surprised.' He took the receiver from her. 'Hello.'

Siana hugged herself and waited tensely for she knew not what. She could hear the explosive crackles over the line, not the words. But when Matthew spoke again his voice was very calm. 'That's quite impossible. And even if it weren't I wouldn't leave now. There's no electricity, no heat except from a fire——' he held the receiver slightly away from his ear and winced at the force of the words coming from it. Then:

'What do you mean?' he asked, and a shiver trickled down Siana's spine at the way he said the seemingly innocuous words. A pause as he listened, then: 'I see. Mentally disturbed, you mean—or would that be as a result of taking those so-called iron pills?'

There was a brief pause. No words. Matthew continued: 'I know exactly what they are. Does that surprise you? Good. I'm glad of that—you'll be interested to know that she's no longer taking them. I burnt them all—except two, which I kept to have analysed if necessary.'

She heard her uncle's voice again, not the words, she wasn't near enough for that, but the tone was possibly different, she couldn't be sure. He spoke for some time.

'Oh yes,' Matthew said. 'I'm staying here—and I'll be here when you return.'

She heard the click, then the burr of the dialling tone. He replaced the receiver, looking very thoughtful. 'We'd better go into the kitchen where it's warm,' he said, 'before you freeze. I've given them a lot to think about.'

'He was very angry. I've never known him angry before.' Matthew took her arm and led her into the kitchen.

'Perhaps it's never been necessary before. I

shouldn't imagine you gave them any cause for anxiety.'

'He said he'd tell the police——'

'I know. He threatened me with that one, told me you were mentally deficient and he'd get me for just about everything. That's why I told him about the pills.'

'What did he say then?' She sat down thankfully.

'Tried to bluff it. Only he knew it wasn't working. Said they were for your own good, and so on. But he knew I had him. They'll be talking now, deciding what to do. Don't be surprised if they cut their holiday short and come home.'

'They'd have a job, wouldn't they?'

'They could get to Glasgow. The airports are open—just; it said so on the news this morning. What they'd do then is up to them.'

'I should never have told them,' she said, white-faced.

'Why not?'

'Because——' she shrugged. 'I don't know.'

'Then don't think about it. I'm looking forward to meeting them, and finding out what makes them tick. And as far as I'm concerned, the sooner the better.'

'Why?' She looked at him.

'You'll know. Soon you'll know.'

He was ruthless—but she had already known that, even before she realised she loved him. And he had a plan and purpose in being there, she was beginning to realise that too. She nodded. 'But I'm not ready to know just yet. Right?'

He smiled. 'Not yet. You're learning fast. I'll make you a cup of tea, we both need one.' She watched him. She might need one, he didn't. Her new resolve had faltered briefly during the telephone call, but now it returned. She had already learned something during the course of that distressing call; she had learned precisely how her aunt and uncle regarded her. As worse than a child. As someone who was not quite all there. To have found that out only days before would have shattered her beyond words. Now, now she could take it, accept it—and know that she was going to fight back. She knew she was sane, she didn't even need Matthew to tell her, although he had. She knew she could cope with whatever happened when they returned. The only thing she wasn't sure about being able to cope with was the fact that he loved deeply— and possibly still did—a woman who had been, and probably still was, his wife. How wonderful it would be to be loved by him, to be utterly possessed and possessing, to have his heart. A warmth, a trembling took her. Dear God, to be loved totally like that. Would she ever know what it was like?

He handed her the beaker of tea. 'Drink up.'

'Thank you.' She smiled at him. She loved him, she was wearing another woman's ring. It would be so easy to pretend—but she wasn't going to. The time for self-deception and pretence was over. 'You've helped me so much,' she said. 'I know now that I can leave here and live my own life, soon.'

'And where will you go?' he asked. 'Have you

thought about that? Do you have any money, for a start?'

'I'll get a job—I'll find something. I couldn't stay here, not now. No, I've no money, but I've a few items of jewellery I was wearing when I——' she faltered—'when I had my accident.'

'Such as?'

'A watch. A good one, an Omega, and a gold bracelet. They should fetch a bit. I'll stay at the Y.W.C.A. for a while.'

'You really mean it, don't you?'

'Yes. I'll keep in touch, with them if they want me to—and with you—if you want me to.'

'That's nice.' She wasn't sure if he was being sarcastic.

Hastily she added: 'Not if you're—moving on.'

'What makes you say that?'

'I don't know. You seem like a man who would travel—you said yourself you'd been all over the place.'

'I might have found the place I want to settle in.'

'Here? At Marine Cottage, you mean?'

'Perhaps.'

She had to ask it. She didn't want to, but she couldn't bear not knowing any longer. 'Is your— wife still alive?'

He looked at her, regarded her very steadily from where he sat at the table. 'Yes.'

She swallowed. 'D—do—you—still love her?'

'Yes.' She closed her eyes. Oh, if only her heart wasn't bumping so rapidly! She felt as if she were going to faint. She shouldn't have asked, she knew that now. But it was too late. There was no way the question could be taken back.

'Forgive me for asking. I didn't mean to. I—I don't know why I did it.'

Matthew stood up. 'It doesn't matter.'

Oh, but it does, she thought. It makes all the difference in the world, and I will have to learn to grow up again like I thought I just had, and it won't be easy. It hurts. It hurts me so much—but you'll never know. 'I hope—you and she get together again,' she said.

'Thank you. You really mean it, don't you?' He half turned, he had been walking away from her, but he stopped.

'Yes, I do.'

He came towards her now. 'Aren't you going to ask me why we parted?'

'No, of course not. I wouldn't dream of asking.'

'But I'd like to tell you.' He pulled up his chair. 'I'd like you to know.'

Didn't he realise what it would do to her, listening? Obviously not. He was a clever, sensitive man, but he didn't know that she loved him. So he wasn't as clever as he thought he was. She shook her head. 'It's perhaps better not——'

'It will help me.'

'Help *you*?' Her eyes widened. That could be almost funny, about anything else. He surely needed no help in anything.

'Yes. She left me because she thought I was having an affair with another woman, a model I'd known for years.'

'And were you?'

'No, I wasn't.'

'Then why——'

'Because Lorna, the model, planned it cleverly for my wife to catch us in what appeared to be a compromising situation. I must have been a fool not to have known Lorna was in love with me—heaven help me, I'd never guessed. When I found out, it was too late. The plan worked—and my wife had gone.'

'But couldn't you have seen her, explained?'

'When I didn't know where she was? I got home and she'd packed and gone. Taken her car and her clothes—and left me her ring.'

Siana looked down at it. That was all he had left of the woman he loved. No wonder he carried it everywhere with him! She felt choked. 'I'm so sorry, so terribly sorry. Did you try to trace her? Her parents—I mean——'

'They'd died the previous year, just before we married. We'd only been married six months, and she was expecting our child.' He stopped suddenly and put his head down, covered his face with his hands.

'Oh God!' The cry was wrenched from her. She reached out to touch him, and she felt closer to him than she had ever done before. She felt part of him, experiencing his anguish. 'Don't go on, Matthew—please.'

He took her hand in his and held it tightly, and she saw something she had never expected to see—the glint of tears in his eyes. 'No, Matthew, no,' she whispered, and knelt before him to put her arms round him, to comfort him. Her anguish was almost unbearable, but his must be more so. She glimpsed, in that moment of his utmost despair, yet another side to his character. He too, was vulnerable. He too had suffered, was suffering.

For timeless moments she remained where she was, kneeling, comforting him, like a mother with a child, soothing, feeling the strength in her, knowing she was succeeding.

'I'm sorry,' he said. 'That was stupid of me.' He looked at her and helped her to her feet, resting his hands lightly on her arms. Something filled the room, a timeless wonder, a knowing; and as it filled the room so something changed, subtly, indefinably, but irrevocably. Life would never be the same again for Siana: she knew that now. Matthew had brought her back to life, had made her see, and be aware, of what the world could hold. For that she owed him her thanks and gratitude. She had also given him her love, but he hadn't asked for that, didn't know it—and now never would. It would be a secret she would keep locked in her heart for ever.

'We're all stupid at times,' she said softly. 'Me particularly. But not any more.'

She mustn't remain standing there any longer with him. She wanted to hold him, to touch his beloved face, to kiss him—but she wasn't going to. She moved away, and the shimmering spell that had held them was broken.

'We'd better light the candles,' she said, 'or we'll be falling over.'

'Tonight we have the lamp,' he answered.

She smiled. He'd said it as though it was a celebration. 'Whatever for?'

'Because. Just because.'

'Very well, the lamp it is.' She watched him light it, and the soft yellow radiance filled the room, like a huge warm circle not quite touching the corners, leaving them shadowy, but enclosing both Matthew and Siana in a soft bright ring of gold.

'Food, and then painting,' he said.

'Painting—in this?'

'Why not? It'll be an experiment. Might be interesting.'

'Indeed it might.'

'And we can talk at the same time—about you.'

'Yes.'

'Just—talk.'

'I know.'

They were having a very simple meal of baked beans and bacon—the last of the bacon, and it was a challenge to make the meals a little bit different each time. Siana added curry powder to the beans, and a few raisins, made hot buttered toast to accompany them, and they feasted, perhaps not right royally, but very pleasantly, and in an atmosphere that had no strain.

After the meal was done and the plates cleared away, Matthew set up a crude easel with the aid of books and board on the table, adjusting the lamp so that the light fell on his canvas, and sat Siana comfortably by the fire with two candles at her end of the table casting a soft glow on her features.

He pronounced himself satisfied after a few minutes of careful adjustment to table, lamp and easel, and began to paint. There was a pleasant silence in the room with only the soft hiss of the lamp, the occasional crackle of wood and coal, settling; she sat quite still, wondering how long it would be before she would need to move, feeling already the slight strain of sitting in one position. He had told her before they began that she was to say if she wanted to stand, to move around for a breather, and she had agreed that she would.

There was no sense of time passing. She could have been there for seconds or minutes when he spoke. 'Siana,' he said, 'move your head very slightly to the left. Just a fraction now.'

She did so. 'That's it. Fine. Comfortable?'

'So far.' She said it almost without moving her lips, and heard him laugh slightly.

'No need to stop breathing, you know. And I'm not doing your mouth yet, so you can talk normally. This mustn't be an ordeal for you, don't forget.'

'It isn't. What part are you doing?'

'Your hair.'

'Oh.' She relaxed fractionally, blinked a few times. For some reason she'd been trying to keep her eyes open all the time, and that wasn't easy. Then she remembered. He had already painted in her eyes; they had been what made the picture instantly recognisable. She wondered if he had ever painted his wife, but she didn't want to ask. Not yet. She didn't even know her name.

'Siana, when we talked before, and you remem-

bered about being sixteen, you told me something
I forgot to note down, but it's been on my mind ever
since. You said, "my parents were old-fashioned,
they didn't really like me having friends". Is that
why you ran away?'

She jerked her head round helplessly to face him,
forgetting the picture, forgetting everything in the
sudden shock of the question. 'Ran away?' she repeated. 'What do you mean? And how did you
know?'

CHAPTER NINE

HE stopped painting, frowning a little. 'I'm sorry. Did I startle you? I thought I'd told you.'

'No. You said nothing, when we spoke about it. All I knew was my life in Manchester, school, and friends—I must have had friends, I remembered their names, didn't I? And I went to a youth club——'

'Your father always met you. You had to be in by ten—you didn't actually talk to any boys——'

'I told you this?'

'It came through, more by what you didn't say. I meant to ask you before—how are your aunt and uncle related to you? Father's sister—mother's brother—what?'

'Aunt Peggy is—was—my mother's sister. They were very close.'

'And presumably alike in character.'

'I suppose so,' she agreed doubtfully. 'But—to say I ran away. Did I tell you that?'

'Siana,' he said gently, 'I took you further than I've told you. I didn't think you were ready then, but you are now. At eighteen you packed your bags and left home to go to London. There was a dreadful scene—it upset you when you told me——'

There was a sudden, electrifying flash of memory,

a glimpse, no more, but Siana jumped as if she had been shot. 'Oh!' She gasped, and put her hand to her head. 'Oh!'

'What is it?' He moved, came over to her.

She shuddered. 'It—something came back when you said what you did. It was like a curtain being lifted aside for just a second—I can't explain it.' She wasn't aware of it, but she was fingering the ring on her right hand as she spoke, and it wasn't until he touched her hand that she realised it.

'That's fine. It's happening as I hoped,' he said. 'And it *will* come as a shock when it happens. You're opening up a part of your mind that's been dormant for two years, remember. And don't you see, your lost memory may be a guilt reaction because you left your home——'

'Guilt?'

'It's easy for parents to make a child feel guilty and ungrateful, to say things like "after all we've done for you, is this the gratitude, the thanks we get?" That sort of thing. It's a shame people don't realise that children have to leave the nest some time.'

She shivered. He was saying words that seemed to have a familiar ring to them. Then she remembered why. 'And in a sense that's what I'll be doing again when I leave here, won't it?'

'Why?'

'Well, they've looked after me, they took me in when I needed help—and it seems that I shall be walking out on them——'

'Because they're stifling you, not letting you be

yourself—as, in a similar way, your own parents did.'

She looked at him. 'I suppose you're right. I *know* you're right. But it doesn't make it any easier.'

'Tell me, how old are they? I've only seen them briefly and casually in the village.'

'Uncle Peter's—um—let me see—about fifty-eight, and Aunt Peggy's a year or so younger.'

'Good grief, you've made them sound as if they were *elderly*! Is he retired? He's a bit young, isn't he, if so?'

'They've got money. Uncle Peter was in insurance years ago, but yes, I suppose he did retire early. I never really thought about it.'

'How long have they lived here?'

'Don't you know?' She gave a cheeky smile. 'I mean, didn't you find that out when you were doing your detective work in the village?'

He grinned. '*Touché!* All right, yes, I do know. I just wanted to see if you did. They've been here about two years. Just about the time you came to live with them, in fact.'

'Oh no,' she looked at him and shook her head, 'you're wrong there, Matthew. Dear me, the famous detective boobs at last! They've been here about ten years.'

He looked at her. The room went very still, waiting, silent——

Siana's heart began to bump erratically, and a *frisson* of something akin to fear shivered up her spine. 'What is it? What have I said?' she whispered, feeling the goose pimples on her arms, and the prickling sensation at the back of her neck.

Matthew sat down on a chair from the table, brushes, painting, forgotten. 'Listen to me, Siana,' he said. 'Your aunt and uncle have lived in this house for two years. They moved in while you were in hospital—you were in for several weeks, remember—and brought you back here when you came out. Now, I want you to think carefully—what have they said to you about how long they'd been here?'

'They said—they just said it had been about ten years—we never talked much about it, it didn't seem important. Matthew, I don't understand—why should they *lie* about a thing like that?'

'I don't know. But I'd like to find out,' he said grimly. 'And, Siana, if you're in doubt, telephone Mrs Patterson. You could phone her about something perfectly innocuous—like has she had any weather reports, your radio's on the blink—then mention it casually.'

'I don't need to,' she whispered. 'I believe you.' She sat back, suddenly tired. 'You'd better tell me any more you know about me. I might as well have all the shocks at once.'

He smiled faintly. 'You think you can take them? There's not a great deal more, yet. You obviously got something when I mentioned leaving home at eighteen to you, let's see if you get any more.' He pulled his chair at a more comfortable angle to the fire. 'You stayed at a women's hostel in South London for nearly a year, and then went into a flat with two other girls who worked in the same office as you—oh, you were working as a secretary by this time for an advertising agency near Oxford Street—any bells ringing yet?' She shook her head. He had known all this, and hadn't said anything. No doubt he had his reasons. The day's shocks were coming fast and strong.

'No. But take it gently. I've had quite a day,' she said.

'I will—very gently. Your social life was looking up. In fact, you were clearly enjoying living in a flat, meeting people in your job, going on holiday with or without the friends, whose names, incidentally, were Jill and Carol.' She repeated them silently. No bells ringing yet. 'You seem to have all got on well together, sharing the chores and cooking, etcetera. Three quite well balanced types——'

'You make it sound unusual!' she cut in.

'No, but there can be personality conflicts with three women sharing a flat. The point I'm emphasising is *you*. *You* were obviously well balanced and mature—get me?'

She nodded. 'Of course. Sorry I interrupted.'

'You're about twenty now. You get a promotion in your job, personal assistant to a director of the agency. Gerald Smythe, I think you told me his name was. Now all this time you were writing home, sending money each week—your parents were comfortably off, by the way, but you felt it your duty—that came over clearly—but they never acknowledged your letters and never wrote back. If you telephoned, they'd hang up. You went home to see why, and there was a dreadful scene that you bitterly regretted having caused. They told you, in no uncertain terms, that you were no longer their daughter, and you went back to London very upset.'

She was shaken by his words. He was right. She wouldn't have been able to bear them before. 'My aunt and uncle never told me anything of this,' she whispered.

'I'll give them credit for that,' he agreed. 'Why upset you unnecessarily?'

'Yes. I see.' She thought about what he had told her for a few moments, and he waited. 'Go on,' she said eventually.

'That's it,' he said. 'And that's enough for you to think about for one evening anyway. Just absorb what I've told you gradually while I carry on painting.' He moved, went back to his makeshift easel and made a few minor adjustments to its position before picking up his palette and brush, and Siana sat very still again. She sensed that he knew much more than he had told her. She sensed it so strongly that it was almost as if she *knew*. But how could she say? She wanted to cry, Stop—I know there's more. What *is* it? But she didn't. She sat very still instead while the chaotic thoughts clamoured inside her mind. Nothing must show on her face, or he would see. Serene and calm outwardly, inwardly a kaleidoscope of images and words, she remained in her seat and waited for him to choose to speak.

'Okay, take a rest. Will you make coffee?'

'Yes, of course.' She did his bidding while he

peered closely at his work, touching it here, wiping with a rag there. 'May I see?'

'Not yet.'

'Oh.' She shrugged and filled the kettle. 'Bossy!'

He laughed. 'Am I? I thought it would be more of a surprise if you don't see it until it's finished.'

'When will it be finished?'

'Oh, another two or three sittings should do it.'

'And then?'

'I'll probably frame it—and present it to you.'

'That's very kind of you.'

'One day, when I'm a famous painter, you'll make a fortune on it.'

She laughed. The conversation was light, meaningless, a polite exchange after tension. One day, he said—one day, when she had gone out of his life and he out of hers—when he, perhaps, would be together with his wife and child. She suddenly felt very empty, an aching, hollow void inside her making her feel almost sick, and it was suddenly no longer funny. She clenched her hands tightly and willed the feeling to pass, and heard him say:

'Siana? What's the matter?'

She had her back to him, so how did he know? She didn't—couldn't—answer him, and the next moment knew he was just behind her, not touching, but close enough to touch, close enough so that she could feel the warm animal heat of him, so that every nerve end in her body tingled with the awareness of his nearness. 'Siana,' he said again, 'tell me.' She sensed his own tension; it reached out to her and enfolded her in an undercurrent of electric awareness that made her heart start to thud. She couldn't move, she couldn't speak. She could hear him breathing, knew he was bending his head, she could feel his warm breath now on her neck, and she was nearly deafened by her own heartbeats. Then he touched her. He touched her, and the world exploded. Wordlessly she turned, and was in his arms sobbing helplessly as he stroked her hair, murmuring over and over again: 'It's all right, Siana. It's all right——'

But it never would be. It would never be all right. Life wasn't simple like that. She ached for him, she longed for him, and he belonged to someone else. Gradually the sobs subsided, tears exhausted, and she stood there in the warm strong shelter of his arms and waited for him to release her. She hadn't the strength to free herself, nor did she, treacherously, want to.

He put his fingers under her chin and tilted it so that she faced him. 'Poor Siana,' he said gently, a smile curving his mouth. 'Poor little girl. I said too much. Forgive me.'

If that were all! Let him think that, if that was what he wanted to. 'There's nothing to forgive,' she said quietly. 'How can you say that?'

'Because it's true. That upset you, didn't it?'

'I'll recover.'

He cupped her face in his hands. 'You really do have the most lovely face. Siana. So beautiful. You are very beautiful.'

How could he say things like that? With one breath telling her how much he had loved—still loved—his wife— and she had even seen the tears in his eyes when he had spoken of her—the next moment telling her she was beautiful. She wanted to hear it—oh, how she wanted to hear it, but it was all so wrong. She moved uneasily, like a small trapped animal, and said: 'You mustn't——'

'Mustn't tell you you're beautiful? Is there some law against it?' he teased.

She shook her head. How to explain? How did you say: I want you to tell me I'm beautiful, I even want you to tell me you love me, because those are the words I want above everything—but not when you love another woman more than anything in the world. Because you don't belong to me, you belong to her, only she doesn't know, and perhaps doesn't care, which only makes it more tragic.

'Let me go, please, Matthew,' she begged him.

'When you've told me why you were crying. We're in this together, or had you forgotten?'

'No, I hadn't. It was a mixture of things,' she said, which was true. 'I just thought of something when you said you'd give me the painting.'

'*That* upset you?'

'No, I felt—empty——' There, it was said. 'Empty inside at the thought of—one day—you said—one day when you're famous—and it seemed as though— it would be some time in the future—and I——' She stopped. She hadn't intended it this way, but it was all coming out, and what did it matter if he knew? He knew everything else. 'And it seemed that it would be a time when—when you and I no longer knew each other.' There, it was done. She waited for his reaction.

The moments passed, and he didn't speak, and the tension, almost a tangible force now, grew and filled the room. She couldn't breathe, and now she could feel his heartbeats, reassuring, faster—or was that her imagination?

His hand moved up her back to hold her more securely, breaking the by now intolerable tension. 'Is that what upset you?' he whispered huskily. She had never seen him so shaken. Not Matthew. Yet it was so.

She closed her eyes. 'Yes.'

'Oh, Siana,' he groaned, 'if only you knew! Do you think I'm going to let you get out of my life?'

'But—but——' What was he saying? He wanted his wife—and he wanted her as well? 'Matthew, please let me go—I don't feel well——' The room had started to spin crazily round, and she was frightened that she was going to faint. She felt her legs buckle beneath her, while a grey rushing wave roared, filling her head. She heard distantly his words:

'I couldn't let you go——' but the words became fainter and fainter, vanishing into the tumble of sound that suddenly overwhelmed her.

When she opened her eyes she was lying in her bed with a hot water bottle at either side of her and Matthew sitting on the bed looking at her.

'I fainted?' she asked.

'Yes. I'm a ruthless swine. I'm sorry, Siana, I

didn't realise you weren't ready to cope with so much—and then making you sit still while I painted you. You should have spoken up before.' It was as though their most recent conversation hadn't happened. Perhaps it hadn't. Maybe it had all been in her fevered imagination.

'Go to sleep now,' he went on. 'An early night will do you good. I shall be downstairs. If you want me, shout, I'll hear you. Goodnight.' He bent over and kissed her forehead in a very brotherly fashion.

'Goodnight.' He went out, leaving the door ajar. In a minute she would get up and get undressed, but it was too much effort, just yet. In a minute....

It was morning when she woke up, and the first sound she heard was a steady dripping from outside. She got out of bed, realising to her horror as she did so that she had slept in her clothes. Then she remembered why.... She must have gone out like a light. She stumbled to the window to look out. The dripping was louder now. She needed a drink before she investigated its source. She went to the bathroom, peeping in Matthew's room. His bed was empty and made up. She frowned and looked at her watch, but it had stopped. Very quietly she walked downstairs.

He was in the kitchen, about to make breakfast from the looks of it. 'Good morning,' he said. 'How do you feel?'

'Fine thanks.'

'I'm getting breakfast. Sit down, tea's made. Do you want the good news or the bad news?'

She groaned and sat down. 'Go on. Good news first.'

'It's thawing. The bad news is—we have a burst pipe.'

'Oh, no! Where?'

'It's all right, I managed to find the stop tap in the cellar. It's the one to the garage—you probably heard it dripping?'

'I did. I wondered——'

'I just turned it off. It should have stopped now. Don't worry, we've still got the toilet and water tap here and in the bathroom. The sun's out and getting stronger. The news said there's a big warm-up all over.' He began to whistle as he made toast with the last of his soda bread. 'Scrambled eggs do you?'

'Perfect. What time is it?'

'Past nine. You slept like a log. No talking, no painting today. We read or play chess, and that's an order.'

Perhaps nothing had happened. Perhaps she hadn't so nearly given herself away. And now, in the cold light of day, it was just as well. Words like that could never be retracted—or forgotten. 'And I'll do some baking as well,' she said. 'Scones and soda bread—and maybe a cake.'

'Why not? It'll be something to feed them with when they get back.'

She had forgotten that. She looked at him. 'Matthew, do you think they will come home earlier?'

'I wouldn't be surprised. I just thought I'd prepare you. They could turn up today.'

'But they've only been gone a week!'

'And so, if they do, doesn't that tell you something?'

She didn't understand him. 'I'm sorry—I'm being a bit dense, but I've only just woken up.'

'If—*if* they come storming home, it'll be for a damned good reason—namely, the fact of me being here has frightened them out of their wits. Now if your aunt phones today, from Canada, and seems to be much as usual, then we—or rather I—was mistaken about them, and I'll mentally apologise.'

She digested his words. 'But you don't think that'll happen?'

'No. Who were they staying with out there? Relatives?'

'Yes. Of Uncle Peter's. No one I know.'

'Hmm. You could telephone, see if they're still there.'

'No, I'd rather not.'

'You'd rather not know. Just wait and see?'

'Something like that.' He handed her a plateful of fluffy scrambled eggs and sat down to eat, after pouring them both tea.

'If they do return, what are you going to tell them?' he asked .

'About moving out?'

'Yes.'

'I'll just say I'm going when the weather's better.'

'No. Listen, Siana. They'll order me out, as they'll have every right to do, and I'll have to go. But I don't want to leave you here.'

She looked up from her breakfast, seeking reassurance on his face. There was none. 'Look, you don't think I'm in danger?'

'Of course not. But they'll work on you—and I won't be here. I want you to leave with me when I go.'

She felt the blood rush to her face. How could he know what he was saying? 'That'll give the village something to talk about——' she faltered when she saw what was in his eyes. 'You mean it?'

'I'm deadly serious. We can go away—anywhere, as long as it's not here. Until you know, that's all. Know exactly *who* you are.'

'I know who I am. You mean until I get my memory—*if* I get my memory back.'

'There's no if about it. You will, I promise.' She had never seen him so serious. 'And you say you know *who* you are. How do you know?'

'What do you mean?' The talk, his words, were leaving her floundering in a sea of incomprehension. Her heart was pounding.

'You think you're Siana Roberts. What if you're not?'

'But I am—I——'

'You might have another surname. You might have been married.'

'Please——' she whispered. 'Please——' she was frightened. 'Oh, dear God, what made you say that?' her voice was nearly inaudible.

'It's possible. Anything's possible. If you stay, you'll never know.'

'Matthew, I want you to take me back—to hypnotise me—now, this morning——'

'No, not yet.'

'But you said—they might return——'

'I know. But wait, until afterwards——'

'Do you know?' she burst out desperately. He didn't answer. He had finished eating, and he got up to take his plate away, and Siana was seized with an impulse she didn't fully understand, and followed him and caught his arm. 'Matthew,' she said. 'Look at me—*look* at me.'

Slowly he turned, looked down at her, eyes dark and deep and unfathomable. 'Do you know?' she repeated. 'Did you take me further than you're telling me?' She shook his arm impatiently.

'Yes,' he answered softly.

'Then tell me, please—oh God, tell me——'

He took hold of her. 'No, not yet. It's not time yet.'

'When—will it be time?'

'When they return. Then, I promise you, you will know. And you will also remember.'

Very gently, almost as if against his will or volition, he moved, and his lips came down on hers.

CHAPTER TEN

FOR a long, wordless time they clung to each other,
and it was a kiss like no other that had ever been
before—deep, explosive, reaching the depths of her
very being, ecstasy. He moved, he murmured something, she knew not what, only that it was right.
This was right. No one else mattered, for nothing
existed save the two of them, and she needed him
so much. He was her anchor, her strength.

'Oh, Siana,' his voice was muffled, lips against her
hair now, teasing, kissing lightly. 'There's so much
to know, but not yet.' His arms were tightly round
her, giving her the strength she needed. Being in
his arms was the only place she ever wanted to be.
Her whole being was suffused with warmth when
he was close to her; she was complete. Away from
him she was like part of a person, not fully alive.
And it was wrong, all wrong. Reluctantly she freed
herself and reached up to touch his cheeks. Tears
were in her eyes. She wanted to say the three simple
words, 'I love you,' but she must not. He caught her
hand and kissed her palm, cupping his own hands
round it. There was a magic in the air that nothing
could dispel, and she knew instinctively that he was
as aware of it as she herself. It showed in his eyes,
in his face, in the very stance of him. A magic, an

eternity in a few moments. All of life was there.

How can I ever live without you? she thought. Without you, I am nothing. It was in her eyes for him to see, and he caught his breath and his face gentled and softened. 'Don't—look at me like that,' he muttered. 'You don't know what it does to me. And I'd vowed not to—touch you again. Not yet.'

Not yet? As if it was not right now, but would be? How could that be? 'You talk in riddles,' she said softly, 'but I don't care.' She was filled with the recklessness of overwhelming love for him. Here, now, he was hers, not some other woman's who had left him. She moved closer again, and stood up on tiptoe to find his mouth. She kissed him, with all the pent-up emotion being released as she clung helplessly, lost to all reason, knowing only this moment, the now that was all that ever mattered. Their bodies fused, melted together in an incandescence that nothing, but nothing, could extinguish. There was an inevitability to all their movements now, a haste, a wanting, a surging desire that overcame all reason or sense.

Somehow they were on the rug in front of the fire, bodies taut with longing, lying closely together while their kisses inflamed them still further.

'This is madness,' he whispered huskily, but it didn't stop him, and Siana, knowing too of the madness that had overcome them, agreed with her mind, but not her body. Then it was too late. As it had always been too late, for ever. And always would be. So how, she thought, as they lay together afterwards, when all was calm and still in the quiet of the room, how can I leave with him, knowing how it will be with us? There was no one to ask her question to, for she could not ask him, for Matthew possessed the madness too, but with him it was a different kind of madness, for he was a man.

She crept away and left him, he watched her lazily, half smiling—and she said: 'I'm going up to have a bath.'

'Even if the water's cold?' he queried lazily.

'Yes.' She didn't care if it was. She just wanted to get away, to think, to be alone. She needed to be alone, to plan her future. For it could not be with him, she knew that, as she had always known it.

Siana baked. She kept herself very busy making just about everything that could be made with the supplies they had—oatcakes, biscuits, scones, a chocolate sponge, using up the last of the cocoa, and a whole tray of jam tarts. It seemed essential to keep physically active so as not to have to think. Matthew sat and read a book, and made sketches on a pad, and they listened to the news every hour, and spoke little. It was as if both were waiting, as if it were a time for silence, for being together, yet alone with their separate thoughts.

The atmosphere simmered with an undercurrent of barely defined tension. Both knew it, yet neither spoke of it. Siana had made a tinned meat and vegetable casserole, and at seven they sat down to eat by candlelight, and she saw his face across the table, in the warm soft glow as he looked at her, and it was all she could do not to cry out. Don't look at me, she wanted to say, not like that anyway.

Can't you see—don't you know what you're doing to me? All she said was: 'More casserole?'

'No, thanks,' he smiled faintly. 'An excellent meal, but with no exercise I find I need less to eat.'

Siana couldn't think how to answer that one, and said nothing. 'Tomorrow,' he said, 'we talk.'

She didn't want to ask what about, and she wasn't going to. 'All right,' she answered. 'Tomorrow.'

She began to clear the plates away, and when he offered to help she refused. 'Help yourself to some cake,' she suggested. 'Or biscuits, or anything you like.'

'I'll have some cake—it looks nice. You did rather a lot of baking, didn't you?'

'I wanted to. No point in wasting oven space when the gas is low.'

'True.' He cut himself a slice. 'Tomorrow I'll try and get the dynamo working again. Then at least we'll have heat, and we can always cook on the fire if we have to.'

'How soon will the snow be gone?'

'A few days. You heard the news. Main roads are being cleared gradually. If this thaw stays, everything should be back to normal within a week.'

But everything wouldn't be back to normal, not as it had been before. What was normal anyway? Her sheltered existence, seeing no one, aware only that the days passed in a kind of blur? She would, at least, never go back to that. And tomorrow they would talk, Matthew said. Would that be the day she would find out, at last? And then what? Escape.

'Then they'll be back.'

'Yes.'

She closed her eyes for a moment, seeing how it would be, trying to imagine what would happen, but she couldn't because nothing like this had ever happened before in her memory. Uncle Peter and Aunt Peggy had never been upset before like they had been during that phone call. Somehow that had changed everything. Tonight she would read the book Matthew had brought, and see if there was anything to help.

She cleared and tidied the table and sat down to read by the light of the lamp. She found it easier to sit at the table to do so, and Matthew sat opposite her, finishing a detective novel she had found for him. She tried hard to concentrate, but his presence made it difficult. Once she glanced across at him. He was totally absorbed in the book, head supported by his hand, elbow on table, face in shadow. His watch glinted on his wrist, everything else about him was dark and shadowed. She watched him silently for a few moments, and he looked up suddenly, as if he knew.

'They haven't telephoned,' he said.

She had forgotten all about it. 'Maybe the lines are down.'

'No. I tried it before when I passed through the hall. It's working.'

'Perhaps they've nothing to say.'

'Perhaps not,' but he smiled as if he knew otherwise.

Siana felt a sudden and totally irrational surge of anger towards him. He had changed everything totally, turned her world topsy-turvy—and he could smile.

'Damn!' She stood up and pushed the book away from her. That had finished it completely. All she could think about now was why they hadn't phoned.

'Perhaps they're on their way here.'

'Very probably,' she snapped. 'But I'm sure you'll deal with them.'

He raised an eyebrow. 'What have I said?'

'Nothing—everything. You don't *care*, do you?' she accused.

'About them? No, not much.'

'About anything!'

'I wouldn't be here if I didn't, would I?' he asked mildly. 'I'd be snug in my little cottage, minding my own business and keeping myself warm— so don't make accusations that are too ridiculous to bother arguing about.'

She had no answer to that, and turned away to look out of the window, breathing hard. He had an answer for everything. And it was so true. He hadn't needed to come; nobody had made him. If it hadn't been for the wallet, though—she whirled round, struck with an idea that was outrageous and at the same time made sense.

'Did you drop your wallet on purpose?' she asked.

He began to laugh. 'I thought you'd never get round to asking.'

'You *did*!'

'Of course I did. And what's your next question?

Now that you're being so logical, there should be another one.' He paused, and waited.

But she didn't know what he meant, and stared hard at him. 'You dropped your wallet deliberately, so that you would have to come back for it. Then— but you didn't plan the snow! Not even you are that clever.'

'No. But I took advantage of it.'

It was terrible. She knew there must be something, yet she had no idea what it was. She had taken the wallet back, and it was snowing but not too badly, and he hadn't been in, but she'd met him coming back—she frowned. What had he said that had made him go back with her? Something about the lights—'The lights!' she said. 'You came back here because of the lights!'

'Well done!'

'But they—you couldn't have switched them off, because it was the——'

She stopped. A suspicion too terrible to voice had suddenly come to her—and she saw his face. 'Oh no——' she whispered. 'Oh no, you couldn't——'

'I couldn't what?'

'The—the dynamo had broken. The *dynamo!*' Horror-stricken, she gazed wide-eyed at him. 'You didn't——'

'Break it? No. Put it temporarily out of action? Yes.'

'My God!' She sat down. 'You mean—all this time——'

'No. Oddly enough, the big freeze up really did put it out of action for me. But you wouldn't have known that because I had no intention of putting it right.'

'That's—criminal——' she gasped. 'It's—it's——'

'It's what? It was the one sure-fire guaranteed way of making sure I stayed here. And boy, did I intend to stay!'

Siana really couldn't take it all in. The enormity of what he had done overwhelmed her. 'If Uncle Peter knew——'

'But he won't, not unless you tell him. And I don't think you will.'

How could she? 'I'm fixing it tomorrow,' he said, 'so it'll be working when he gets back. House cosy. Have *you* been cold? Have *you* suffered in any way?'

She was only half listening to him. The whys clamoured in her head for attention. Why? Why? *Why?* Why her? Why the elaborate and cunningly devised plot to get him there and keep him there? Because it had all worked like clockwork. And all because, he said, he wanted to help her get her memory back. And he wanted to make love to her, and had certainly succeeded in that. But there were easier ways to get a woman, surely?

'Why—me?' she gasped. 'And if you say, you'll know soon enough, I'll scream!'

Matthew shrugged. 'Then I won't say it.' He looked at her in silence instead. She found that more disconcerting than his words had been.

'I should hate you for this,' she breathed.

'The interesting thing is that you say "I *should*"—

not "I do",' he remarked. 'I'm making progress after all.'

'Who are you?' she demanded. 'Who are you—really?'

'Matthew Cra——'

'No, I don't mean your name. I'm sure that's real enough. I mean *you*—who, what are you, and where are you really from?' She looked at him, her eyes wide with the fear of the unknown, because that was suddenly what he had become, an unknown force, a man from nowhere, who was no longer what he seemed to be. 'You frighten me, you frighten me terribly.' The last few words were said in little more than a whisper.

'Oh, no, Siana, that's the last thing you should say.' He spoke equally softly, all banter gone from his face and voice. 'You are safer, and more protected now, with me, than you have been for a long, long time.' He looked at his hands, he lifted them slightly, as if in supplication towards her. 'I would no more hurt or injure you in any way than I could myself. You're safe, so safe, but you don't know it.'

'How can I believe you?' The words were wrenched from her, and the tears were in her eyes. 'How can I believe anything you say any more? I don't *know* you.'

'Not know me? When we've lived here together these past days, been together in the fullest sense of the words, have shared laughter, and sadness—and you don't know me? When we've looked at

one another, and known what the other was thinking—and have shared the magic that came from
just being here together—dear God, Siana, what
do I have to do to prove that you have no need to
have that fear of me in your eyes? Do I have to say
what's in my heart, in the very depths of my being?
Do I have to tell you what I feel about you? Will
you then believe?'

She was shaken. His words were all she had ever
wanted to hear, but wrong, so wrong, because of the
other woman's ring that she wore. How could he
love two women? A wordless cry escaped her, and
she ran out of the room fumbling, stumbling in
the darkness, anything to escape what mustn't be
said, sobbing as she found her way up to her room
and slammed the door behind her. She sat in a chair
huddled in her eiderdown, shivering, knowing she
mustn't stay there too long. But where could she
go? Where was there to escape?

She heard Matthew call her, telling her not to
be stupid, to go down before he came up to fetch
her, and still she sat there, numbed, not moving,
her mind a confusion of thoughts and pain. She
heard his footsteps in the hall—and then a thunder-
ous knocking at the front door. She heard the door
being unbolted, a car driving away, then a voice,
an angry, almost hysterical woman's voice. Her
Aunt Peggy.

CHAPTER ELEVEN

SIANA listened to the voices from the hall with a kind of growing horror. The anger came up at her in waves of sound, of shouting, a man's voice, a woman's shrill tones—the quieter ones of Matthew were nearly lost. She crept to the door and opened it with freezing fingers. Trembling, she leaned against the wall. The unbelievable had happened: they had returned. It was just another shock to follow on what had already gone before. She couldn't stay there; she had to go down and face what was there to be faced.

She threw the eiderdown off and felt her way along the hall towards the stairs. The voices had faded, but the argument continued in the kitchen. The anger vibrated from there.

Siana lifted her chin and walked in. Instant silence fell as three pairs of eyes turned to her. Aunt Peggy, large in fur coat, silver hair still touched with snow, glasses slightly askew; Uncle Peter, his face white with temper, looking explosive and dangerous. And Matthew, standing big and calm. It was at Matthew she looked first, saw what was in his eyes, and nearly went dizzy.

Now, again, she saw another facet to his character. There in the dim light, he seemed to have grown in stature. He dominated the scene because he, he alone, was not angry. It made him all the more overpowering.

Aunt Peggy spoke first. 'Siana, this man is to leave here at once!' She came over to where Siana stood at the door, her face shaking with the rage she couldn't suppress. 'How dare you—how *dare* you have a man here while we were away!' She looked angry enough to strike Siana, who stood her ground, the violent force of the rage in the room hitting her in a wave. But she stood there and looked at her aunt, then her uncle, and said:

'I'm sorry, but I couldn't have managed without him. He's helped me——'

'Helped you!' Uncle Peter stepped forward, took hold of Siana's arm and dragged her forward. 'You little bitch——' he spat, and Siana cowered, seeing the dreadful, *awful* uncontrollable rage on his face. 'You should be beaten——' He got no further. His arm was struck upwards by Matthew, who had moved so swiftly and silently that none were aware of his action until it happened.

'Touch her again and I'll break your arm.' He meant it too. Uncle Peter clutched his arm which appeared to be numbed, and backed slightly at the force behind Matthew's whiplash words.

Aunt Peggy swung her heavy handbag at Matthew. 'Don't you touch my husband!' she shouted. He raised his arm, deflecting the bag as if swatting a fly, caught it and took it from her, dropping it on to a chair.

'This ridiculous screaming won't get anyone anywhere,' he said, deadly calm and icily controlled. 'We'll talk like civilised adults.'

'In *my* house you won't,' spluttered Uncle Peter. '*You'll* leave—and *now*.'

'If I do, I'll take Siana with me.'

There was an instant silence at his words. No one moved. It was like a tableau, a frozen scene in a waxworks. Siana spoke into that vacuum.

'*If* you make him leave, I shall go too,' she said. She walked over to the cooker. 'I'm going to put the kettle on and make us all a cup of tea, and we'll drink it and talk.'

She saw the look exchanged by the older couple, but she felt no triumph, only a sickness that it should be like this. If Matthew had shocked her, they had shocked her more, far more. The look had said it all—Siana's different. I am, she thought, but at the moment I don't feel pleased about it. She filled the kettle and as she did Matthew spoke.

'Why don't you sit down?' he said. 'You might as well be comfortable to hear what I've got to say. And I do have a lot to say, and most of it you're not going to like, but I don't intend leaving until it's said. There's no way you can make me leave— either by words or force.'

The couple listened. Uncle Peter didn't give up easily, you had to hand that to him, thought Siana. 'You stand in *my* kitchen and tell me what to do?' he snapped, his temper barely under control. 'If that doesn't indicate your character I don't know what does.'

'I don't give a damn either way what you think

about my character,' Matthew retorted equably. 'But I might take issue with you over whose kitchen it is—or even whose house it is, come to that.' He smiled at them both, and it wasn't a pleasant smile.

Aunt Peggy picked up her bag and sat down as though her legs had given way, and after a moment Uncle Peter did the same. 'What do you mean?' he said after a moment and quite quietly.

'I think you already know. And if I hadn't been certain before, I would be now,' answered Matthew. He pulled up a kitchen chair and sat straddled, elbows resting on the chair back. 'I've been doing a lot of hard work over the past few months—detective work, you could call it, and I know why you've kept Siana nicely sedated, why you pretended you'd lived here for ten years when it was more like two——' Siana listened numbly, not understanding. Yet clearly both her aunt and uncle did. They were both whiter, and very quiet, all temper gone and in its place—shock. Aunt Peggy's fingers twisted and tugged at her handbag strap and her mouth had a pinched look. Siana handed her a cup of tea, then one to her uncle. Matthew's and her own she put on the table.

'Are you—are you from the police?' Uncle Peter asked.

What was he saying? What did he mean? The police—as though he were *frightened*. It was all going horribly awry.

'No. And I'm not a blackmailer either.'

Siana spoke then. She couldn't stand not knowing any longer. They did. She was the one person in the room who didn't know what was going on. 'Matthew,' she begged, 'what does all this mean?'

He looked at her. 'I'm sorry, Siana. You above all have a right to know. You weren't ready. You were learning too much about yourself to take in more. It's quite simple. Your aunt and uncle are not entirely the kindly couple you thought. They did you out of a substantial amount of money, which enabled them to buy this house. The fact you'd lost your memory was the key factor. If you hadn't, the money would have been yours—and you might well all have been living in this house, but under different conditions—they as your guests.'

She looked at her aunt. 'Is this true?' she whispered.

Aunt Peggy bit nervously at her lip. 'We knew you wouldn't mind,' she said, 'And when you recovered your memory we were going to explain.'

'Only you made pretty certain she wouldn't by doping her with those so-called iron pills, and keeping her out of contact with other people who might have accidentally triggered off her full recovery,' said Matthew grimly.

'We meant well,' Uncle Peter cut in. 'We've looked after her, cared for her, loved her like our own daughter——'

'And treated her like a mental defective,' cut in Matthew. 'Which she isn't, wasn't, and never has been. That's more wicked than anything else you've ever done.' His tongue lashed them relentlessly. He looked at Uncle Peter as he spoke. 'As long as you were safe, that was all that mattered. Oh yes, I know all about your 'retirement' from the insurance company. It was that or prison, wasn't it? You were able to repay what you'd embezzled, they didn't want any fuss—bad for the image—and you moved here. I know everything about you—I made it my business to.'

'What are you going to do?' whispered Siana's aunt.

'Nothing. It's not up to me. It's for Siana to decide whether she wants to throw you out of *her* house. All I want is a chance for her to lead a normal life, with her memory intact. And for that reason I'm getting her out of here. She's coming with me to my house tonight. Tomorrow she can decide.'

Siana looked at the middle-aged couple, who seemed to have shrunk slightly. 'I'd never do that,' she said quietly. 'I still don't know what's going on, but I wouldn't—even if it is my house—see you homeless.'

'Who are you?' asked Uncle Peter dully, a different man from the one who had stormed his way into the house.

'You'll know, soon enough. Siana, go and pack some clothes. We're leaving here tonight.'

She looked at him, picked up the torch, and went quietly out. She heard him continue speaking as she left the room. 'We're going to my house, Marine Cottage. We'll be back here tomorrow to sort everything out——' His voice faded as she made her way up the stairs. She couldn't take any more shocks. She just wanted to sleep, she was so tired. There couldn't be any more surprises. There couldn't possibly be more.

She flung underwear, sweater and trousers in a holdall and made her way downstairs.

She knew instantly, as she entered the kitchen, that something else had happened. She knew it by the waves of shock that carried across from the two shattered people by the fire, by the way—the *dazed* way they looked at her.

Matthew smiled as though everything was utterly normal. 'Ready?' he asked.

She looked from them to him. 'What——' she began.

'Later.' He looked at her gently. 'Later. When we get home.'

Neither Uncle Peter nor Aunt Peggy looked up as she walked towards the door for her coat and wellingtons. They looked as if they were in a state of shock. So am I, thought Siana, but now I'm learning to become immune.

Matthew opened the door. He already had his coat and boots on, the duffel bag, with his precious radio in it over his shoulder. 'Let's go,' he said.

Siana looked at them. 'Goodbye,' she said. They looked up, but they didn't answer. She looked wordlessly at Matthew, and he took her arm.

'Let's go home,' he said quietly. 'We'll talk there. Not here.' He closed the door quietly behind them, and in the cold air outside took Siana's bag from her, his free hand supporting her arm. 'Come on, love,' he said.

*

She needed his support on that endless journey to Marine Cottage, how she needed it. There was no time to speak, they had to concentrate on making their way through rapidly melting, slushy snow, and she was cold and exhausted when she reached there. Matthew's first job was to sit her in the kitchen and switch on both oven and gas rings to their highest. 'Stay there,' he said, 'while I light a fire and get you warm.' She sat in a daze, hardly taking in any details of the small crowded kitchen in which she sat. It was a man's room, with no concession to feminine taste. Fishing tackle, an outboard motor from his boat in one corner, wellingtons, a cardboard box full of tools. Yet it had an atmosphere she liked, because it was his, and he part of it, and his personality was stamped on it. She was getting warmer. He pushed a glass in her hand. 'Drink that,' he said. 'It's whisky.' She sipped, and felt herself thawing, like the snow outside, becoming warmer gradually and, as the whisky took effect, more contented. Because, in spite of everything, this was the place she wanted to be: with him. It was no palace. It wasn't dirty, but it was untidy, and casual, and totally masculine, and she loved him so much that nothing outside the four walls mattered any more.

The fire was crackling nicely now as he flung dried twigs and branches to feed it, and the room was warm and light with the paraffin lamp on the table. She turned to him and looked at him, and he grinned at her and came and bent over her.

'Cheer up,' he said. 'It's nearly all over now.'

'I'm cheering up. I'm probably tipsy as well, but I like it.'

'Want a cup of tea?'

'No, thanks. This'll do me.' She hugged the glass as if he might take it away from her. Matthew laughed and ruffled her hair, then kissed the top of her head lightly.

'Just stay there till you're quite warm. The fire will be going properly in a minute, then you can get your coat and boots off and sit by it.'

'I don't even know what I'm doing here,' she said, revelling in his touch, the touch of his mouth on her hair, and the warmth of him. 'You just told me to come, and I did.'

'Yes.' He took the glass from her, put it on the table, pulled her to her feet, and put his arms round her. 'That's the way it's going to be.'

'Oh, Matthew, you know—you must know by now how I feel about you—but it's not——' He put his finger on her lips.

'Ssh! All will be explained shortly.' He grinned down at her, and there was something in his eyes that she saw shining out for the first time, then the grin died, and his face was very serious, but it was still in his eyes, that which she had known she would see. And still she didn't understand. Because what she saw in his eyes was love.

She made a little sound in her throat, a mixture of joy and anguish, and searched his face hungrily, beginning to know, beginning at last to realise, but not daring to even think about it, because it would be too bizarre——— 'Matthew?' she whispered. 'Matthew?'

'Yes?' a mere breath of sound in return.

'What is it? Tell me.'

'I think you're already beginning to know. I think——' he touched the end of her nose gently with his finger. 'I think you're either beginning to get your memory back, or——' and he smiled, 'or you're beginning to read my mind.'

Her mouth trembled. 'What I'm thinking is too fantastic to put into words.'

'Is it any more fantastic than everything else that has happened these last few days?'

'Much, much more.'

'Then try me with it. You never know, do you?'

'It can't be——'

'Nothing's impossible. What is it you're thinking?'

'No.' She shook her head. 'I'm going crazy—and it's that whisky as well——'

'Come and sit down.' There was a small settee by the fire, very old, of leather, and comfortable-looking. Matthew moved a couple of books and pushed her gently down, then sat beside her. He put his arm round her and said: 'Now we'll talk. You're ready now. Just say what's in your mind.'

Siana began to trace a pattern on her knee, aimless circles, and he put his other hand over hers and stopped her. 'Go on,' he said.

'I can't. I just can't.'

'Then I'll help you. Why don't you ask me my wife's name? You never have.'

Eyes wide, she looked at him. In a moment she would know. And did she, now, want to? What if it weren't——'

'What is your wife's name?' she asked, the words less than a whisper.

'Siana.'

She thought she was going to faint, and it was as if he knew, for he held her tightly, turning her towards him, both arms going round her. 'It's you, my dearest love, it's you.'

Of all the tumult and shocks and surprises of the last days, none could now be counted as anything. This, this, was far greater and more earth-shattering than her wildest dreams could have envisaged. She began to tremble helplessly, hopelessly, and Matthew held her as if to give her the strength she needed to begin to realise, at last, the final truth of all. The one truth that made everything else fall into place.

Faintly, she whispered, 'Oh, Matthew, my darling love, my very dearest—oh, how I love you! When I knew at last, just minutes before, when something came to me that made everything seem sense, I was so frightened——'

'Frightened? Why?'

'Because—it might have been wrong, and then my whole world would have collapsed.'

'Is that how much you love me?'

'Don't you know?'

'I want you to tell me.'

She began to laugh, softly, happily. The reasons for all that had happened, the complications, the unhappinesses, all faded in the light of what she now knew. 'Oh yes, yes, *yes*, I love you. I've loved you almost from the beginning—but it's grown and grown until, suddenly, I was frightened. You remember when you were telling me how much you loved your wife?' He nodded. 'I hurt, I ached—I hated her—how could I do otherwise? I didn't know it was me. Oh, dear God, I didn't know. I never realised—not then.' She smoothed her hand over his face, revelling in the touch of him, wanting to hold him close, to be with him always. 'And when you—we made love, I knew it was wrong—I thought I knew,' she corrected herself, 'but I was beyond caring about right and wrong. There was always something, with you, something in the way you looked at me, but I was too blind—or perhaps not ready—to see. Really, you know the whole story, don't you? You've known all along.'

'Yes. But I had to do it gradually, to ease you into the knowing. Do you remember anything yet?'

'Traces. Fragments of something, with all the shocks.' She touched her ring lightly. 'This—this helped. It was mine, wasn't it, of course?'

'Yes.' He took her hand, eased the ring from her finger, then, taking her left hand, put it on her wedding finger. 'I'm returning it to where it belongs.' He bent to kiss it. 'And there it will stay.'

'I left you—oh, Matthew, how could I have?' she was anguished.

'The model I told you about, Lorna—remember me telling you?' She nodded. 'I was working late one evening in my studio. She had some urgent photos to be taken for a magazine, a rush job. I didn't know she'd phoned you. She timed it right she waited until she heard you letting yourself in the studio and stripped—she was modelling bikinis—and grabbed me. You walked in at the precise moment she did so. She'd told you in the call—disguised voice, of course, for you'd met her once or twice—that I was having a wild affair with one of the models. What you saw seemed to confirm it. You dashed out—she clung on to me screaming hysterically that she loved me——' he stopped, clasping his hands tightly together so that the knuckles showed white. 'God help me, I had to slap her face hard to stop the hysterics, bundle her into her coat and get her out. By then you'd gone, in the car. My studio was a mile away from our house. I ran all the way, but you'd gone, leaving your ring.' He stopped and touched her face lightly. 'And that was the last I saw of you, from that dreadful night to one day four months ago, when I saw you again walking along the beach. By that time I'd not only traced you, but I'd also found out all about Uncle Peter's activities, his resignation—and why—from his firm and the move here. You'd told me when we first met in London—your advertising agency boss was a friend of mine, and introduced us, by the way—that your parents had recently died in a car crash on their way back from holiday in Canada.

'There was money to come to you from the estate of your grandfather, your father's father. You didn't know how much, then. Your parents had never forgiven you for leaving home, and you'd imagined it would be something in the region of five or six thousand.' He paused. 'During the course of my detective work to trace you, I found out it was much more. It took me eighteen months to find you, Siana, and when I did, I moved here and I waited, and I listened, and talked, and asked casual questions, and began to piece the jigsaw together. I bided my time, because I knew that one day when I knew everything there was to know, I was going to have you back.'

'But you didn't know they'd be going away, did you?' The whisky had made her calm, and dreamy, almost as if she were listening to a story about some-one else. It was perhaps better that way. It didn't hurt so much to hear facts that at another time could hurt deeply. She had been so foolish and so very mistaken. And so much time had been wasted, so much time. . . .

'No. When I found out, I made my plans. Even if they hadn't, I had something arranged. And noth-ing would have stopped me.' He smiled. 'Do you want to know what it was?'

'Yes.'

'Kidnap.'

'What!'

'Simple abduction. All neat and tidy, get you back here—go and tell them who I was, what I knew about them, then come back, and show you all the photographs of us both, and make you see——'

'You have photos of us?'

'Yes. I used to take them, remember?' He

laughed. 'But I didn't need to, because the glorious opportunity came when on the village grapevine I heard the news of their intended visit to Canada, leaving you alone. Incidentally, doesn't it strike you as a bit of a coincidence that your parents were killed in Canada? Are you sure your uncle was visiting *his* relatives?'

'They said so—what——'

'I don't know. But your grandfather Roberts was a Canadian. They could have gone over for more money from his estate. You'd signed over powers of authority when you were in hospital, to them. Which would explain their having to go, even if it meant leaving you alone behind, here. You see, your aunt could sign on your behalf—and also, presumably, bank any money due to you.'

'I don't want it,' she said dully. 'I don't care. They can keep the house——'

'I know how you feel. In a way I agree, but don't let them get away too easily. It's unimportant anyway, my love. What matters is you. And I've got more than enough to support you, and me—and our children—for the rest of our lives.'

'Children,' she whispered. 'Matthew, I was pregnant, wasn't I?'

'Yes,' he said softly. 'Two months——' his voice broke. 'I've been to the hospital you were taken to after the crash—you lost it. I checked the records——' he kissed her. 'I'm sorry, darling, I don't want to hurt you——'

'It's all right.' She turned to him, eyes very bright with unshed tears. 'Soon—again——'

'I know.' He smiled. 'Soon. Very soon.'

'If not already,' she murmured, and a warm tide of colour suffused her face. 'Is there more?—I'm very tired.'

'Very little. The extra pieces can be sorted out tomorrow. It's been like a giant jigsaw so far. But we've all the time in the world to complete it.'

'You told them, didn't you, when I went to pack?'

'Yes. You knew. That ended all resistance to your leaving.'

'Was I on my way to them when I was—running away from you?'

'Presumably. They're your only relatives. They lived in Glasgow——'

'Until two years ago?'

'Yes.'

'I don't hate them, even in spite of all they've done—I could never hate them,' she whispered.

'I wouldn't want you to. They've been foolish, they've robbed you, but they've learned a lesson tonight that they'll never forget.' He stood up and pulled her to her feet. 'And now, Mrs Craven it's time for bed.'

'Mrs Craven,' she repeated. 'So I am! I'll have to get used to it, won't I?'

'It won't take you long.' He held her to him closely. 'Give me an hour or so and I'll make you forget you were ever a single woman.'

She suddenly remembered something that had been in her mind for a day or so, and looked at him, the beginning of an impish smile at the corner of her mouth. 'Matthew, before we go—before you

make me forget everything else—that first time—
we——'

'Mmm?' he murmured, and he knew, but he was
going to let her ask him, and he was laughing.

'Your back—and the fever, and the delirium—
was it—was it real?'

'What do you think, my sweet?' His eyes told her
the answer.

'But——' her eyes widened, 'it was so genuine!
I mean—I touched your face, your forehead—you
were clammy—how?'

He caught her tightly to him; he was shaking
with laughter. 'Oh, Siana, I had a cup of cold water
under the bed. Each time you went out, I dabbed
my face and hands with it——'

She was laughing too, now. 'And your back?'

'Not strictly a lie there, my darling. I did hurt it
once, long, long ago in rugby—the memory of it
helped me.'

'You devil! I was frightened you were going to
die——'

'I know. But I was prepared to go to any lengths
to get the real Siana back. It worked, didn't it?' He
began to stroke her face gently. 'But now, I think,
we should make up for lost time.'

'And we have *all* the time in the world,' she
murmured, as he closed the door softly behind them
and they began to climb the stairs.

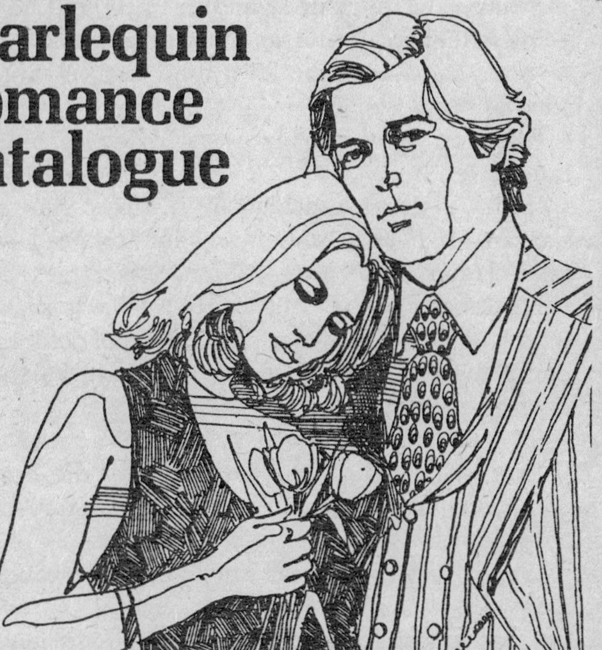

Harlequin's Collection . . .

Many of these exciting romance novels have not been
available since their original publication.

Harlequin Presents...

Stories of elegance and sophistication . . .

Harlequin Romances

. . . and be sure not to miss any of these
exciting novels.

Don't miss any of these exciting titles.

Complete and mail this coupon today!